What People

Praise for *The Best c*

"The story grabbed me from the first paragraph and would, I think, do the same for most teens and 'teens at heart.' A novel that retains its authenticity to this degree is rare and should not be missed."

Christian Week, author Fay S. Lapka

"The book is a pleasure to read... Not only is this book entertaining but it also teaches young adults a lesson in life."

Christian News Ottawa, reviewer age 18

"Get several copies of this book. It's a winner!"

Resource, editor Rick Hiebert

Praise for *With Friends Like These* (Book 2)

"Lindquist combines the angst of growing up with the need for an increasing relationship with God... Draws the characters with skill and warm insight."

Christian Library Journal

"Struggles with jealousy, petty pride and romance—the stuff of life at any age, but of particular importance to young people learning their way in the world.... That's Life! Communications has a winning series in hand..."

Christian Week, editor Doug Koop

Praise for *A Friend in Need* (Book 3)

"One teenager helps his friends—and even a couple of his enemies—deal with their problems in a Christian manner, and in the process learns a few valuable life lessons himself."

Provident Bookfinder

"Although intended for a teenage audience (12-18) this book... might well be enjoyed by adults of any age."

Christian Library Journal

"This vivid novel for teens presents relationships, struggles, and the search for love and for God. Real issues are dealt with, and Christian solutions provided."

Catholic Insight

"A good read for teens faced with a friend in a wheelchair, or who use one themselves."

David Hudson

Praise for _More Than a Friend_ (Book 4)

"Glen Sauten captured our sympathies as we rooted for him to stand up and discover himself.... Lindquist has found the teen voice, but writes to the emotional needs of all ages."

Stephen and Janet Bly, authors of over 100 books

"I recommend the Circle of Friends novels to every teen I meet."

Linda Hall, award-winning author

"N. J. makes Christianity and Christ come alive."

Joel Comiskey, author and speaker

"A master story-teller, Lindquist will hook you with the first couple of paragraphs and keep you reading."

Deborah Gyapong, author, journalist

The Best of Friends

Book 1 in the Circle of Friends series

The Best of Friends

Book 1 in the Circle of Friends series

N. J. Lindquist

That's Life! Communications

Markham, Canada

The Best of Friends

Digital book ISBN: 978-1-927692-02-8
Print book ISBN: 978-1-927692-03-5

Published by That's Life! Communications
Third Edition. First published in 1991 by Moody Press and in 2000 by That's Life! Communications

New Cover Design 2022 by Best Page Forward.
Circle of hands by maxstockphoto on Shutterstock

This novel is a work of fiction. Names, characters, locations, and events are the product of the author's imagination and any resemblance to actual persons, locations, or events is purely coincidental.

Published by That's Life! Communications
Box 77001, Markham, ON, L3P 0C8
Email: comments@thatslifecommunications.com
thatslifecommunications.com

The author's website is njlindquist.com

Dedication

For all the teens I've worked with over the years.

While my characters and my stories are pure invention, you inspired me to write my books.

Chapter 1

Luke's text said, "Not this weekend, Glen. Taking Jamie to the movie tonight."

"We haven't been there all summer. This might be our last chance."

"Sorry. Taking Jamie shopping in Stanton tomorrow. And there's a party tomorrow night. What can I say?"

No more explanation needed. I was getting the picture. "Okay. See you at school Tuesday."

"Not coming to the party?"

"Doubt it. And you'll be too busy with Jamie to talk to me anyway."

"I don't spend every second with her."

"Sometimes it seems you do."

"You're crazy. Hey, I didn't see the time. Got to pick up Jamie up at the hairdresser's. Later."

I put down my cell phone and made a face at it. I'd known when I texted him that it was a long shot, so I wasn't surprised.

So there were only four days before school started, and I didn't have a single thing to do.

Last year, Luke and I drove to Willard's Peak and stayed for the weekend in his tent. But I'd barely seen Luke in over a month, ever since Jamie Ramsdale broke up with Tyler Stevens and Luke broke all speed limits stepping into Tyler's shoes.

Personally, I think Luke is crazy. Jamie's the kind of girl who demands all your money, all your attention, and all your time. So what if she's the head cheerleader and the most popular girl in the school? Anyway, with taking her shopping, helping her baby-sit, buying her fancy coffees, and generally hanging around her all the time, Luke had lost contact with all his old friends, including me.

I decided to walk over to Ed's Pool Hall and see if there was any action. Small towns are pretty dull, especially in the summer.

Mom was busy in the kitchen, so, since I vaguely remembered her having asked me to do something, I quietly headed for the front door.

"Glen!"

How does she do it? Mothers and teachers seem to develop the ability to see through walls! Or maybe they just read minds.

"Yeah?" I replied, my hand on the doorknob.

Mom came into the living room. She was holding a big, round, white plastic container. "Glen, where were you going? I asked you to take this across the street for me."

Despite the fact that she was wearing denim shorts and a sleeveless pink blouse, she looked flushed from baking on such a warm day. I felt a twinge of guilt, so I reached for the container.

She jerked back, out of my reach. "Glen! You can't carry it that way! It's an angel food cake. Don't you remember my telling you?"

I grinned. My memory has never won me any awards. "Nope. Where'm I s'posed to take it?"

She walked to the window and I followed her. "All right. Do you see that brown and white house over there?"

"Sure," I replied confidently, "Hastings."

She sighed. "They moved out last week. Remember?"

"Nope. Guess I wasn't too interested. They were old enough to be my grandparents." I thought of my fashionable grandmother. "Great-grandparents, maybe."

"Mr. and Mrs. Hastings moved to the city to be closer to their son and his family. And yesterday, while you were out fishing, a new family moved in. The Thorntons. He's a doctor and he's going into partnership with Dr. McGrady. I think there's a boy about your age."

"Now, carry the cake from underneath, like this." She started to give it to me and then stopped.

"You need to comb your hair first." She frowned. "You'd better change your shirt, too. You seem to have managed to spill some of your lunch on it."

If I'd had more energy, I'd have argued. Instead, I went to my room and rummaged through the drawers until I found a clean T-shirt. Then I had to look for a comb. I finally found one on the floor near the bed.

Mom and I both have this sort of wavy but not quite curly brown hair that does pretty much whatever it wants no matter how often you comb it. I needed to get a haircut, because the longer it is the more of a pain it is. Mom keeps her hair fairly short for the same reason. I ran the comb through my hair and it stayed pretty well the same, but at least I could say I'd tried. Let's face it, I'm not much in the looks department. I'm about five-foot-ten with a few muscles and ordinary features—nothing that stands out. But I don't scare little kids when I look at them, either.

I put the comb on my dresser and went out to get the cake. Mom made me use both hands to take the plastic case from underneath. Then she held the front door for me. As I started down the sidewalk, she called out a final, "Do be careful."

I grinned back at her. Then I felt annoyed. She had no reason to talk to me as if I was eight years old; I was seventeen, and going into my final year of high school.

I made it across the street without dropping the cake, and soon I was at the door of the Thorntons' house. I was trying to balance the cake in one hand so that I could ring the doorbell with the other when the door opened and a guy about my age started out, then stopped and stared at me.

Embarrassed about holding a cake, I stammered something about my mother having baked it and he flashed a big smile, then held the door open for me to go in. He called to his mother, and a tall, slender, blond woman in a bright red skirt and jacket came to take charge of the cake. She said she'd go right over and thank Mom for it, so I pointed out which was our house, and then she took the cake to the kitchen.

I stood looking up at the boy who, at about six-foot-two, had the biggest shoulders, the blondest hair, and the widest smile I'd ever seen.

He spoke first. "Name's Charlie. Charles, really, but Charlie sounds friendlier." He stuck out a large well-tanned hand and I grasped it. His grip was painfully strong.

"Glen Sauten," I mumbled back. Then I didn't know what to say.

"You go to high school?" he asked eagerly.

I nodded. Then, feeling more was expected, I added, "Grade twelve. How about you?"

"Same." If possible, his smile got wider. "So, is there anything to do around here? Maybe if you're not too busy you could show me around?"

"Sure," I replied enthusiastically. "Er—that is, we could walk downtown. It's only eight blocks." I felt my face get flushed—the way it always does when I say something dumb.

"Walk?" His laugh started in his stomach and worked its way up. "Charlie Thornton never walks! Come on. I'll show you how we get downtown."

I envied the way he just left without his mother coming to see where he was going or asking him to do something first. We went into the garage and Charlie, with a flourish, opened the passenger door on a gleaming red Mustang. I got in.

With a bow, he shut the door, then walked around to the driver's side. In no time, we had backed out of the drive and were on our way.

I leaned back, relaxing against the soft cushions. This was the life. "Hey, this isn't yours, is it?"

"Sure it is. I may trade it in on a newer model, though. Dad got me this one when I turned sixteen, so it'll soon be two years old."

I couldn't believe my ears. This guy'd had a new Mustang for two years, and my Dad wouldn't let me buy a two-thousand-dollar Ford after I'd saved the money? Unreal!

We stopped at the pool hall, and I took Charlie in. A couple of friends of mine, Matt Robertson and Brandon Lovansky, were there. They're both in my grade, and I've known them forever.

Matt is fairly short—about five-foot-seven, and skinny, with reddish-blond hair and a face full of freckles. Brandon is about my height, but he's a lot bigger than me. According to his doctor, he's about thirty pounds overweight. But Brandon doesn't worry about it.

Anyway, they're both good guys. Nobody you'd notice, just ordinary good guys. They've lived next door to each other all their lives, and they've been best friends all that time. And they've been friends with Luke and me nearly as long.

After I made the introductions, we had a few games of eight ball. Charlie was the winner and I ended up on the bottom. Pool never was my game.

Loser was supposed to buy Cokes, so the four of us went over to Harry's Restaurant and I blew most of my ready cash.

While we were there, I learned something more about Charlie. The four of us were in a booth and Charlie was telling stories about the city where he used to live, and asking us what it was like to have lived in a small town all our lives, when I realized we had become the focus of attention for nearly every girl in the place.

Not that they were really obvious about it, but still, they were having a good look. Now, I knew it wasn't me they were interested in, and I didn't think it was Brandon or Matt, so that left Charlie.

He seemed to be ignoring them.

Finally, Brandon and Matt said they had to be going or they'd be late for dinner. We watched them go. Then Charlie got up, slowly, and I followed.

"Don't forget the bill." He nodded toward the table.

"Huh? Oh, yeah." I grabbed it and paid at the counter.

Meanwhile, Charlie went over and started to talk to the prettiest girl in the place. Not wanting to butt in, I stood at the counter, pretending to read a notice that was pasted on the glass. They looked over at me once and Sophie, a redhead who was also in grade twelve, shrugged. Finally, Charlie came over and we headed out the door. As we got in the car, I kept myself from being nosy. After all, I'd only known the guy for a few hours.

We drove home and stopped in Charlie's driveway.

"I hope you aren't busy tonight," he said as I reached for the door handle.

I stopped, then looked at him. "Huh?"

"I said I hope you aren't busy tonight."

"Tonight?"

"Yes."

Sure I was busy. First I was going to watch television. Then I was going to read the paper. Or maybe I'd read the paper first and then watch television. Or I could do both at the same time. "Not anything important," I replied.

"Good. I'll pick you up at seven-thirty and we'll take in a movie."

I had to laugh. "In this town it's *the* movie."

He laughed, too, and I got out and headed across the street, hoping Mom wasn't holding dinner for me.

She was, of course. She often did. Sometimes for Dad, but usually for me. I have this habit of forgetting to look at the time. I think she tries extra hard to be nice to me so I'll feel bad. Like waiting dinner. Sounds nice, but she always manages to say something like, "The potatoes were even better until I had to warm them up," or "The meat got a little greasy while I was keeping it hot." So it sounds like, because of me, everyone's dinner is spoiled.

Not that you'd ever know it, though. If for no other reason, my mom could go down in history as a great cook. Of course, I was the sixth kid she'd had to practice on, so by now she could do it with her eyes shut.

While we were eating roast potatoes, fried chicken with biscuits, broccoli, and lettuce salad with home-made dressing, Mom said Mrs. Thornton had dropped over to thank her for the cake and that she seemed nice. Apparently, she's an interior decorator and since there isn't much scope for her talents in Wallace, she planned to open a store in Stanton and drive back and forth. Stanton's a small city half an hour west of Wallace.

Then Mom asked if I'd met Charlie.

"Yep," I replied as I stuffed in another forkful of potatoes.

"Don't talk with your mouth full," Dad said as he reached for seconds. I hope I have the same tendency to stay skinny as he does—because he eats as much as I do.

"She asked me," I mumbled.

"What was he like?" Mom asked.

"Okay." I continued eating.

"Can't you expand on that a little?" Dad asked in his slightly impatient tone. I think he sometimes wonders why, after five intelligent, capable kids, he had to finish up with me.

I reached for more milk. "I guess so."

"Well, what about him?" Mom asked.

When I didn't reply right away, she added, "Is he your age?"

"Yeah."

"Did you like him?"

"Sure."

"Will he be in your grade?"

"Yeah."

"Was he friendly?"

"Yeah."

"Were you?" Dad said with a smile. "Or did you even speak to him?"

I looked up, set my fork down, and grinned, "They could use you two down at the police station. Yes, I was friendly. And I spoke to him. In fact, I spent the afternoon with him, and I'm going to the show with him tonight. I will also confess that he has a two-year-old Mustang, red, with a white interior, a radio and CD player, and a lot of horsepower. He is over six feet tall, with blond hair. He seems to be very popular with girls. And he beat me at pool. Anything more?"

Mom smiled. "Thank you for—what is it—'squealing' to us. And doesn't everybody beat you at pool?"

Dad nodded. "You may as well take your money and throw it in the nearest creek as play pool. I've never seen anybody so bad."

I gulped down my third glass of milk before answering. "Nice to have parents who defend you. What's for dessert?"

Mom took a pie—apple—out of the oven, and I put cheese on it.

After we'd finished eating, she told Dad and me to go play some Ping-Pong while she cleaned up. Never ones to argue, we scrammed to the basement before she changed her mind.

Dad wanted to bet a dollar a game, but I refused— said it would be too much like taking candy from a baby, me being the baby. And, anyway, I'd spent all my cash that afternoon. He won three games in a row, so we called it quits and sat down to watch TV.

Almost immediately, Mom was yelling that someone was there for me. I remembered that Charlie was coming at seven-thirty and looked at my watch. Seven-twenty-nine. I took the stairs two at a time.

I could hear voices in the living room. Charlie was saying things like, "Very much, Mrs. Sauten," and "I'm certainly going to enjoy living here." I paused in the doorway. I'd changed my T-shirt after lunch, but I'd worn this one all afternoon and during dinner. Mom wasn't beyond sending me to change right in front of Charlie. I ran to pull a clean shirt out of my drawer and slip it on.

Charlie was sitting, perfectly at ease, talking to Mom about where he'd lived before. I was immediately glad I'd at least changed T-shirts. Charlie was wearing a pair of brown cargo pants and a brown and orange sports shirt.

When I came into the room, he jumped up, said he was pleased to have met Mom, and led the way to the door.

I gave directions on how to get to Sophie's. Although she lives on the other side of town, there are only about two thousand people altogether, so it's just a few minutes' drive.

We soon found her parents' red brick house. This was the "old but good" section of town. We also have "old but okay" and "old and grungy" sections, besides the newer ones like where Charlie and I live.

We parked in front, and Charlie got out. He started toward the house, then stopped and looked back at me. "Well, come on."

Surprised, I said, "That's okay. I'll wait here."

Charlie stared, then grinned. "Don't be an idiot. Both girls are here. Sophie said her friend lives down the street and would come over. Hurry up."

He went on, and I had to follow.

I was an idiot, all right. It had never occurred to me that Charlie would fix me up with a date. I'd gone places with Luke all the time, and if he took a girl I did the driving.

The only time I'd ever dated a girl was some Sadie Hawkins dance when she'd asked me. And then it had been Lottie Perkins, the dumbest girl in class. I didn't want to go, but Mom blackmailed me.

It isn't that I'm afraid of girls or anything. I've just never felt any real desire to get to know them. I mean, I'm doing okay without them. I'm only seventeen—plenty of time left. Why, my dad didn't get married until he was twenty-six! That gives me nine more years.

The door opened.

"Oh, Charlie, I wasn't sure you'd actually come," said Sophie, giggling between every word. "I wondered if maybe I'd just dreamt I met you at Harry's." She took a few steps forward and then squealed. "Oh, Charlie, is that your car? It's gorgeous!"

Ava Porter had come out behind Sophie, and when Sophie introduced her to Charlie, she stared, giggling. Then, rather pointedly, Sophie said, "And here's *your* date, Ava. You can come closer, Glen. She doesn't bite."

Ava is a tiny blond who follows Sophie around. She's okay, I guess, but I've never said more than two words to her in my life. Nor did I ever intend to say more.

I coughed, mumbled something—don't ask what— and was relieved to hear Charlie say, "Let's go," to the girls.

In a few seconds, I was in the back seat of the Mustang with Ava. Fortunately, she joined in the conversation between Charlie and Sophie, and I was free to sit back and relax.

When we got inside the theatre, I pulled out my wallet. Uh-oh. I had about eighty cents.

Charlie was paying for his and Sophie's tickets.

"I—er."

"Problem, Glen?"

"Sort of. I forgot to get more money."

He laughed

"No worries," he said, handing me two twenties.

I told him I'd pay him back the next day, but he said not to bother. I just shook my head.

We found seats in the back row of the theatre. Charlie sat on Ava's other side, so I didn't have to talk to her. In a way, it was just as if Charlie had brought two girls, and although I had a hunch it bothered Sophie, it sure didn't bother me.

I saw Luke and Jamie. They were at the back on the far side. They were totally preoccupied with each other.

The movie wasn't bad—some kind of detective story and war story combined. I forget what happened, but there were two really good chase scenes. When it ended, Ava asked Charlie if he'd been to the Peabody Diner yet, and of course he hadn't, and he'd love to see it.

So we piled back into the car, and both girls gave directions. We got there eventually. In a town the size of ours, you'd get anywhere eventually.

A lot of cars were already parked around the tiny building. The Peabody Diner is just a local joint, owned by an older couple named Smith who take off for a few months in the winter and shut it down. I guess if we were on any kind of major road, we'd have had a chain burger place like McDonalds or Burger King by now, but because we don't have any major highways nearby, we're still stuck with local joints. Of course, if we have a hankering for chain food, we just have to drive to Stanton. They have one of everything.

The Peabody Diner is a small restaurant with only three tables inside. But it has a large parking area and some outdoor picnic tables. Most people eat in their cars or at the outdoor tables.

The girls wanted milkshakes and French fries, so Charlie and I got out to get them. He offered to do it, but I needed the fresh air.

We had to walk by a carload of girls, and you could hear them giggling. One of them leaned out and said, "Hi, Glen," in a very friendly tone. It was Marta Billings, someone else I've known my entire life.

When we were little, I think we played together a bit. But she got kind of weird as she grew up. She has coal black hair, which she wears long and straight, and she dresses mostly in black pants and baggy black sweaters and she wears a lot of make-up. On the whole she looks—well, kind of scary.

I think this was the first time in years she'd spoken to me other than to tell me to get out of her way, or to whisper some sarcastic comment when I gave a wrong answer in class.

I ignored her. If she wanted to meet Charlie, she'd have to do better than that.

"Friend of yours?" Charlie asked.

"No," I replied truthfully. "We mutually can't stand each other."

Charlie laughed as we got into one of the two lines at the counter. "How can you not stand a pretty girl?"

"Marta? Pretty?"

"Is that her name? Marta? I like that. You'll have to introduce me. But later. Not in front of Sophie and Ava."

I didn't say anything, because a couple of the girls who had been with Marta in her dad's car had come up behind us. Kayla and Emily are okay—not totally weird like Marta, but nothing great either. Standing behind us in line, they acted as though they didn't even know we were there, but you could tell they did. They were just making themselves available in case we—or rather, Charlie—wanted to talk to them.

Apparently he didn't. He talked to me about cars—mostly his—and then asked about our school's football team. Fortunately, we have one, and not a bad one, either. Maybe having a lot of strong farm kids helps. We finished second in our league last year and lost a heartbreaker in the playoffs. Charlie sounded really interested. But just then we got our turn at the counter.

Charlie did the ordering. Since it was a busy night, there were French fries already cooking, so we got our order in a few minutes.

Sophie and Ava were giggling about something when we got back to the car. They wouldn't say what. Charlie started teasing them and they lapped it up.

Girls are—well, I've only known one or two who don't act silly. I guess they're okay, but they sure get strange around guys they want to impress.

But Charlie didn't seem to mind. In fact, he seemed to be acting just as silly, only in a different way. I couldn't be bothered—even if I knew how—and even if Ava was the least bit interesting.

So I drank my milkshake and ate my French fries and enjoyed watching the three of them.

At a little after eleven-thirty, Sophie reluctantly said she had to go home soon. There was a dance the next night, and her dad wouldn't let her go unless she was home by midnight tonight. So of course Charlie asked about the dance.

I thought he was going to ask Sophie to go with him, and I think she did, too. But he didn't.

We took the girls home. Charlie parked halfway between Sophie's and Ava's houses, so we each walked our date to her door.

Charlie and Sophie went hand in hand. Ava started off in the direction of her house. I followed.

"Nice night," I offered.

"Yes."

A pause. "Movie wasn't too bad, huh?"

"I guess so."

I went on for a few steps before realizing I was alone. I turned.

She slowly caught up. "Are you a good friend of Charlie's?" she asked. "Did you know him before?"

"Nope. Just met him today."

We were walking together now.

"Where did you meet him?"

"At home. He lives across the street."

"Oh." She thought it over. "So he doesn't know anyone else yet?"

I caught on to what was going through her mind. Should she be friendly to me or wait until Charlie got settled and maybe chose new friends?

She must have decided not to take any chances, because she smiled. "Well, it certainly was a nice evening, Glen. Maybe I'll see you at the dance tomorrow?"

"Maybe."

"This is where I live." She stopped. "Well, good-night Glen. See you tomorrow."

"Yeah."

I waited until she'd gone in. That's what Luke always does. Then I wandered back to the car to wait for Charlie.

I sat in the car for about fifteen minutes before he showed up. He was whistling as he got into the driver's seat.

"So, Glen old buddy, what do you think?"

"About what?"

He laughed. "Ava, of course. Any good?"

"Good for what?"

He laughed again. "What a joker! Good for what! Hey, Sophie's not bad. Not bad at all. Nice house, too. And her dad's a lawyer. Good family, and good-looking. I just might give her another call soon."

I didn't say anything. If he wanted to date Sophie that was okay with me. Just as long as I didn't have to.

We were on our way by now, but instead of heading home we went back to The Peabody Diner. Marta's car was still there, and Charlie drove up behind it and got out. He looked at me through his open window.

"You coming?" he asked.

"Where?"

"I thought we'd get some girls for tomorrow. What's her name again? Martha?"

"Marta."

"Yeah. How about it?"

"Uh, well, you go ahead. I'll wait."

"What do you prefer? Blond, brunette…?"

I cleared my throat but my voice still sounded hoarse when I said, "None."

Charlie laughed. "No preference, eh? That's how I feel, too. Give them all a chance."

"That's not what—"

An annoyed female voice interrupted me. "I don't know why you've stopped here. There are some empty spaces. And I'd like to back out." It was Marta.

Chapter 2

Charlie paused just long enough to wink at me before he turned to face her. He hooked his hands into his belt loops and leaned against the Mustang. He took his time, looking her up and down before drawling, "Well, hi there."

She put her hands on her hips. "When are you planning to move your car?"

"When I'm finished what I came for."

"Which is?"

"Well, I thought maybe you and one of your friends might like to go for a drive tomorrow afternoon. I'm new here and I haven't seen much of the countryside yet. Maybe you could show me around?"

"Why should I?"

"Why shouldn't you?"

"I don't know if I want to."

"I can only take three passengers. One of my old man's rules is one to a seat belt."

"That's only three."

"You forgot my buddy Glen here."

She stared into the window. "You mean Glen Sauten?"

"That's right."

"If you say so."

"Any complaints?"

"No. He just doesn't seem your type."

"How about you?"

"He's not my type, either."

Charlie laughed. "You know that isn't what I meant."

She crossed her arms and looked at him closely. "Maybe. What time tomorrow?"

"Two o'clock."

"You want two of us?"

"The more the merrier."

"Well, I'll see. Where will we meet you?"

"How about if you come to my place at two? You know where Glen lives? Well, I'm just across the street. And, by the way, my name's Charles Thornton. You can call me Charlie."

"Marta Billings."

"See you tomorrow, Marta."

Charlie got back in the car and in a moment we were on our way home.

"Say, you didn't have any plans for tomorrow, did you, Glen?"

"Naw. I quit work Wednesday so I could goof off a couple of days."

"Yeah? Where'd you work?"

"Grocery store. Filling shelves and carrying stuff. And deliveries."

"All summer?"

"Yeah."

"Well, you need some relaxation then. We'll meet the girls at my place. Go for a drive. Take in the dance at night. These dances any good?"

"Okay, I guess."

"Many girls come alone?"

"Some."

"So we'll go stag. Might find something interesting."

We pulled into the garage and got out of the car. I said good night and started for home.

"Hey!"

I turned.

"I plan to work on the car in the morning. Come on over if you aren't busy."

"Sure." I waved, then headed for home.

The key was in its usual place in the mailbox. I'd tried carrying one, but after I'd lost three, Mom decided to do it this way.

It was dark inside, and quiet. But as I went past Mom and Dad's room, I heard a soft whisper. "Glen, is that you?"

"Yeah, Mom."

"Did you and Charlie have a nice time?"

"Sure."

"That's good. See you in the morning."

"Yeah. Night, Mom."

I went into my room and got ready for bed. It had certainly been an interesting evening. And tomorrow we were going out with more girls. Up to now, my life had been fairly dull and ordinary—but happy in a quiet way. I had a vague feeling that having Charlie here was going to change my life. Whether for better or worse I just didn't know.

Mom woke me the next morning. She had a list of about ten things I could do around the house to help her with the fall cleaning. My sister and her husband and their two little kids were coming in the afternoon and staying till Monday, so all the work had to be done by noon.

It was twelve when we stopped for lunch, so I didn't get near Charlie and his car. I'd looked over once and he was busy washing it.

Janice and Ron and the kids arrived just after one. The kids are cute. The older one is three and the little one is just beginning to walk. I don't mind looking after them so long as I don't have to change any diapers.

Ron and I had them in the back yard when Mom came to tell me that Charlie was out front with a car full of girls. Ron started making cracks, but I grinned at him and took off. To tell the truth, I'd have rather played with the little kids, but having told Charlie I'd go with him, I thought I'd better go.

Marta was sitting with Charlie in the front seat. Emily was in the back. They'd left room for me on the right side.

The two girls kept up a continual flow of talk with Charlie, so I was free to sit back and enjoy the ride—which I did. I like seeing all the fields and the farms and the ponds and groves of trees.

We'd been driving about half an hour when Marta said something I didn't hear that got Charlie laughing. It must have been about the car because he suddenly gunned the motor and showed us what the engine could really do. Emily started screaming, but Marta was laughing and urging him to go even faster.

The road we were on wasn't that great—a two-lane gravel road. If there happened to be a car ahead of us, we would have to pass, and if there were any cars coming

toward us at that moment, well, that would be too bad
for us and them, too. And being a country road, there
was apt to be a tractor or a slow-moving farm truck on
the road.

"Charlie," I yelled, "slow down!"

He immediately dropped down to just a little above
the speed limit. "Just showing Marta what this baby can
do." He smiled.

"Well," I said, "this isn't the best road to do that on."

"Scaredy-cats," Marta said, her eyes dancing.

"I need to go to the bathroom," Emily said. "Now."
She giggled. "That'll teach you to drive so fast."

Marta and Charlie started laughing.

I stared out the window.

It was about fifteen minutes before we found a small
village with an old grocery store and a dirty-looking garage that had a small cafe at one end. We went in and
the girls took turns going to the tiny one-stall bathroom.
We bought drinks and surprisingly good doughnuts, and
took them outside where there was a single well-weath-
ered picnic table. We sat around and talked and laughed.
Okay, *they* talked and laughed; I listened.

When the food was gone, we piled back into the car
and drove around some more. Charlie kept pretty much
to the speed limit; the girls talked to each other and him;
I was able to relax and enjoy the scenery.

All in all, it wasn't a bad way to kill an afternoon.
Charlie and the girls were kind of entertaining, the food
was okay, the car was great, and I always like being in
the country. Dad says the stork goofed and I should have
been delivered to a farmer instead of a bank manager.

We got back to town just after five. I said I'd go with Charlie to the dance, and he said he'd pick me up around nine—no sense being early.

For once, I was on time for dinner. It was another good one—roast pork with baked apples, baked potatoes, and green beans, topped off with Mom's lemon pudding. Ron kidded her by saying next time he and Janice had a fight, he was going to run home, except he'd run to his mother-in-law instead of his mother. Then he had to tell Janice she was almost as good a cook. So what with joking and eating and doing dishes and looking after the little kids and just plain having a good time, I forgot all about Charlie and the dance until he knocked at the door.

Dad answered and asked Charlie in. He had on a pair of shiny black pants and a pink shirt with a white sweater. Mom took one look at my jeans and hustled me off to the bedroom. Between her and Janice, they found a pair of khaki pants and a blue shirt made of some light material—don't ask me how I got it—and made me change.

When I got back, Charlie was talking to Dad and Ron, and they all seemed to be enjoying themselves. But Charlie jumped up when he saw me.

We were half way to the car when Mom called me back to give me a sweater. Where she'd found it, I don't know. I think it's one my grandmother gave me last Christmas. At least, I remember she gave me a sweater, because I'd been hoping for an iTunes gift card.

As far as dances go, I guess it wasn't half bad. There were a lot of kids there, having one last bit of fun before school started. Personally, I've never been much on dancing. Maybe it's good exercise, but I'd as soon jog. So any time I go to a dance, I find a few other guys who think like me, and we have a good time telling jokes and talking about cars and sports and just watching everybody else jump around as though a bunch of fleas had been let loose on them.

This time wasn't much different. Charlie got me to dance once with some girl—I think it was Mary Lou—so he could ask the girl she was with—Peggy. But after that I figured he could manage by himself, so I left him to it. Every so often he came over to ask me about someone, or I saw him on the floor and he waved. He seemed to be having a good time dancing with every girl in the place.

Two of the people he asked me about were Luke and Jamie. Okay, he was more interested in Jamie. I looked at her, trying to be objective. She's about five-foot-seven and very athletic, but with curves in all the right places. She's done a lot of gymnastics, and makes a great head cheerleader, but she also does track and swims. She has short, straight black hair, cut in what I think is called a pixie look. She isn't what you'd call beautiful, but you do look at her when she's around. She knows how to use makeup, and she always seems to act a few years older than she actually is. Anyway, Charlie was interested.

"Nope," I said. "She's one girl you should forget about. She and Luke are going together. Luke wouldn't like it if you tried to cut in."

"So who's this Luke?"

"Well," I said. "He's sort of my best friend. I expect you and he will be friends, too. He's good at sports, and he's got a car he looks after like it was a baby, and—well, he's a nice guy."

We both looked over where Luke was dancing a slow one with Jamie. You had to admit that they made a good pair. Luke's about six feet, with a very muscular build from working out with weights a lot and playing several sports. His hair is as dark as Jamie's, but very curly. He wears it in sort of a fifties look, with sideburns. His skin is dark, like he always has a tan. He usually wears jeans and a black leather jacket, so I guess some people would say he looks like a motorcycle gang member. But a very good-looking one. He's probably the most popular guy in town, and Jamie's the most popular girl, so it's sort of right they should be going together.

"So you wouldn't like it if I stole his girl, huh?" Charlie said.

I started to say, "as if you could," but held back. So far as I knew, Luke had never had trouble getting or keeping girls. But then, he'd never had to go up against Charlie.

Anyway, for now Charlie seemed content to dance with every other girl who was there, including Sophie, Ava, and Marta, each of whom seemed to want him to spend more time with her and less with the others. I saw quite a few dirty looks aimed at the backs of other girls.

I managed to introduce Charlie to Luke and Jamie, but other than that I didn't get a chance to talk to Luke. He and Jamie were never more than arm's length from each other.

I had a reasonable time talking to Matt and Brandon and some other guys, so I guess we were all satisfied.

I thought Charlie might want to take a girl home, but he didn't. We gave Matt and Brandon a lift, then were home ourselves by one o'clock. Charlie asked me what we could do the next day. We settled on tossing a football around in the afternoon since Charlie wanted to sleep in.

Ron and Dad woke me at seven in the morning to go golfing. That was fine with me. Golf is one of the few games I can almost hold my own in. We had a quick breakfast and then managed eighteen holes before lunch.

Mom had barbecued a chicken, so we ate out in the back yard and had a real good time. When Charlie came, Ron said he'd like to toss the football with us for a while, so we went to the street and took turns punting and catching.

Charlie was good. He said he'd been a quarterback the year before, and since I knew our top quarterback had graduated, there was definitely room for him to make the team.

After we'd worked up a sweat, Charlie and I went to the The Peabody Diner for drinks, but there wasn't much action. He wanted to drive around and find some girls in the evening, but I said I thought I should stay home because Ron and Janice were there. He seemed disappointed, so I asked him to come over because we'd likely play some games, but he said no thanks; he'd drive around by himself. So I didn't see him again until the next afternoon.

It was Labour Day, and the stores were closed. Janice and Ron left right after lunch, and Mom suggested I walk over to see if Charlie wanted to toss the football for a while.

I knocked on the door and after a few minutes Charlie answered. He said he'd been listening to music and asked me in. He had a complete home theatre right in his room, with all the latest equipment—plus a huge music and movie collection. He also had more clothes than I'd know what to do with, a whole wall covered with trophies and ribbons, and another wall covered with pictures of girls.

We listened to music for a while, and then my cell phone rang. It was Luke. He and some kids had decided to have one last fling at a small lake about half an hour away. They were going to drive up for a wiener roast, then swim or play baseball.

Charlie wanted to go, so I told Luke we'd be there. Since we had Charlie's car, we offered to drive some other people and Luke said he'd call back and let us know.

Charlie found his bathing suit and towel and his baseball glove, and then we went out to the kitchen to see if there was anything we could take along. His folks were out, but he found a couple of bags of salt and vinegar chips and some pretzels. Luke called back to say it was a go, so at five-thirty we loaded ourselves in the car and went to pick up Brandon and Matt.

When we got to the lake, Luke and Jamie were building a fire, so we all pitched in and soon had a good one blazing. The girls unpacked the food and Luke opened the drinks. All in all, there were about twenty-five or thirty kids there—mostly from grades eleven and twelve, with a sprinkling of younger kids and a few who'd graduated in the spring.

I found Charlie helping Sophie put a frankfurter on a stick. Ava was waiting. Marta came up with her stick. "You'll have to help me, too," she said. "I can never get them on right. They always fall into the fire."

Charlie laughed. "You'll need to get in line."

Marta's lower lip broke into a pout.

Charlie laughed again, but after he got Ava's stick ready, he put an arm around Marta and helped her.

"Now how do I keep it from falling off?" she asked.

"I guess I'll just have to help you."

"I need help, too." Sophie almost put her stick into Marta's face.

"Be careful!" Charlie said. "I'll help both of you."

"And me." Ava wasn't going to be left out.

I shook my head and wandered over to Matt and Brandon. If Charlie wanted to spend his time with weird girls, that was his business. But ten minutes in their company made me feel a bit queasy.

We ate until we were stuffed, and then just sat around for a while. A couple of the guys think they're comedians, so they entertained us. Charlie got in the act, and he had some funny stories, too.

A few kids went swimming, including Luke and Jamie, who did a few laps together and pretty well ignored everyone else.

The water was cold, so most of the girls didn't go in past their knees. But they got a lot of exercise yelling and squealing and running in and out. Personally, I'm not much for swimming. I'd as soon lay on an inner tube and just float around. But Charlie was the real thing. He was diving off the raft and really enjoying himself. Of course, any of the girls who hadn't yet met him couldn't help getting interested. He's just that kind of guy.

Later, we got two ball teams organized and had a pretty good time. As usual, I got stuck out in right field, but I don't mind. I can just enjoy the fresh air and the breeze—Like I said, I should have been born on a farm. Charlie, though—he started out on second base and ended up pitching after the other team had scored eight runs in two innings.

After that, we won. They got four more runs, mostly because Charlie pitched real easy to the girls, but we got fourteen—with Charlie being involved in a good many of them.

Luke and Jamie were on the other team, Luke at short-stop and Jamie at third.

Neither of them likes losing, and I heard them arguing about a missed ball and a bad swing. I also saw Luke give Charlie a look that said, "I'll remember you."

After the game, we went back to the fire and roasted some more marshmallows and finished off the drinks, and by the time we'd packed up it was after ten.

A few kids wanted to stay longer, but we still had a half hour drive home and tomorrow was the first day of school, so most of us thought we'd better head back.

Several girls looked longingly at Charlie's car, but Matt and Brandon and I got in and we had a good drive back, telling jokes and talking about the evening and laughing. We didn't drive too fast, so it was eleven by the time Charlie and I pulled into his drive. I said I'd pick him up for school in the morning. When I got home, I got a short lecture about being in bed by ten-thirty on school nights. Mom wasn't really mad—just keeping in practice.

Tuesday morning, I called for Charlie at twenty-five to nine. Mom had dragged me out of bed and seen that I was on time. He wondered about taking his car, but I said it wasn't worth it today, and besides, it was only a few blocks. So we walked.

He wanted to know about the teachers, and I told him about the ones I'd had before. I thought there were a couple of new ones this year, so I didn't know about them.

Then he wanted to know about girls—were there any he hadn't met yet? I really couldn't think of any. Well, just a couple who I didn't think he'd be interested in—one dumpy girl who never takes part in anything, and Zoey Burgess, who wears glasses and is kind of chubby and sort of plain. Girls seem to like her, but I've never noticed any guys that were at all interested.

And then I remembered *her*. Why I hadn't before, I don't know. She's everything Charlie could want, and no doubt she'd like him, too. At least, she might. With her, you never can tell.

Charlie noticed that I'd stopped talking. "What are you thinking about? Remember somebody?"

I didn't know whether to tell him or wait until he spotted her himself. I decided to wait. "Nothing special. If I've missed anyone, you'll soon find out."

Chapter 3

At that moment, we turned a corner and the school came in sight. Charlie forgot about girls and started to laugh. "That's it?" he said. "It's so small!"

Wallace High School is next door to Wallace Elementary School. Both schools are gray one-story buildings built with concrete blocks and flat roofs about twenty-five years ago. I guess they were state of the art at the time. Now they're kind of depressing. But then, what school isn't depressing?

Apparently, the school Charlie went to before was a sprawling two-story building with over 2,400 students. Our high school is lucky to hit 400. About half of them come by bus from farms and villages in the area.

When Charlie was through laughing, we headed for the front doors and he followed me down to room ten. That's the room for seniors who are academically inclined. The other two senior rooms are for those who plan on going into a trade and those who are taking the commercial program.

Charlie had told me he wanted to be a doctor like his dad, so it was easy to see why he was in the academic class. Why I was there is a different story. My dad made me. I wanted to take the easier course because, well, it's easier. Not to mention that my grades have never been anything to brag about. But Dad said every other one of his kids had gone to a good college and he'd be hanged if I wasn't going for at least a year, especially since I have no idea what else I want to do. So, there I was. I'd told Dad that if I failed, it would be his fault.

Anyway, we went into the room and found desks about half-way up. Charlie's idea—I prefer the very back. We talked with others until the bell rang and Mr. Jackman came in. Everyone sat down.

I'd already told Charlie about Mr. Jackman. He's stout, about fifty, nearly bald, with small beady eyes. He smiles occasionally, but not much. His kids—two boys—are both grown and doing well. His wife is a friend of my mom's and one of the prettiest and nicest people I know. But Mr. Jackman is neither pretty nor nice. Of all the teachers I've had over the years, he's the one I really listen to. His is the one class I never daydream or talk in. Not that I like history—I don't. But no one fools around in Mr. Jackman's classes. Not that no one ever has. But if you've done it once, you don't do it again.

So now, everyone quietly sat down. We've never had him for home room before, but it looked as though we were stuck.

He started calling the roll, and it was then I realized that two of us were absent. Not entirely absent, because there were notebooks on two desks near the front. But the desks had no one sitting in them, and he didn't call out their names; he simply made a mark in his book.

He'd finished the roll and was starting to give us our timetables when the door opened and two girls came in carrying books. They took the books to his desk and he nodded as they left them there and went to their seats.

Charlie was behind me. He poked me in the back and whispered urgently, "Who is that?"

"Which one?" I countered, knowing that nobody in his right mind would care who Zoey was.

"The blonde, of course."

"Oh, her. I thought you meant the brunette. Let's see now. The blonde, eh?"

He poked me again.

"Oh, yeah, I remember. Her name is Nicole."

Mr. Jackman frowned at me, and I tried to pay attention to what he was saying.

Charlie waited a few minutes and then poked me again.

I leaned back as far as I dared.

"Her name is Nicole?" he whispered.

"Yeah." I mumbled, "Nicole Elizabeth Grant."

I sat up and began taking down something Mr. Jackman was saying.

Charlie poked me again, but I ignored him.

A few minutes later, I looked over at Nicole. She was wearing a green skirt with a matching sweater and her long golden-blonde hair shone against the green like a field of wheat against a forest of trees. As always, she was smiling as she looked at Mr. Jackman. I couldn't see her eyes, but I knew they would be smiling, too. They always are. In my opinion, Nicole's not only the prettiest girl in the school, but the nicest too.

And it seemed to me from the past three days of observation that Charlie was going to be number one among

the male population—at least as far as the girls were concerned.

But there was just one small thing. Nicole isn't that
interested in guys. Oh, she dates now and then, but I
know for a fact that she's refused to go out with Luke and
most of the other guys who'd had enough nerve to ask her.

I couldn't help wondering if she'd refuse to go out
with Charlie. I had a feeling that if she did, he wouldn't
shrug his shoulders and find someone else the way Luke
had. No, the more I thought about it, the more I decided
that Charlie's presence in town was definitely going to
add some interest to my life.

Charlie finally quit trying to get my attention, so it
wasn't until Mr. Jackman had finished his instructions
and we were looking at our timetables that he got a
chance to talk to me.

He kept his voice low. "Her name is Nicole?"

"That's right."

"Do people call her Nicki?"

"No."

"Nicole Grant?"

I nodded.

"How come you didn't tell me about her?"

"Forgot, I guess."

"You forgot *her*?"

I shrugged. "Ask my mother. She'll tell you my memory stinks. Are you taking physics?"

"Yeah. But how come I haven't seen her before? Why
wasn't she at the dance?"

"I'll tell you later. Rats, I hate having chemistry so
close to lunch!"

Charlie gave me a dirty look, but he paid some attention to his timetable and then started talking to Marta and Sophie and a couple of other girls.

After a few minutes, a bell rang and it was time for the first class. Since most of us were taking history, we just stayed put and Mr. Jackman gave us a preview of our history course and told us what else we'd need for it. The bell rang again and we went on to more twenty-minute classes—the teachers just saying their names and handing out books and telling us in general what we'd be doing and what we'd need. Before long, it was time to leave. School would really start the next day.

Charlie and I were barely out of the building before he was bombarding me with questions about Nicole.

"All right, who is she and why haven't I seen her before today?"

"I told you—Nicole Grant."

"Keep going."

"What do you want to know?"

"Why haven't I seen her?"

"Because she's kind of different."

"What do you mean?"

"Well, I don't think she's ever been to a dance—town or school. I've only seen her at a couple of movies—one was a Walt Disney matinee and the other was a movie her dad's church sponsored.

"Church?"

"Yeah. Her father's the minister at a church in the new area northeast from where we live. They moved here about three years ago."

"So she goes to church, does she?"

"Yeah, her whole family does. And, like I said, I've never seen her at a dance, and she doesn't go to many movies. And she doesn't ride around in cars much, either. There are a couple of guys she dates now and then, but I think they go to the same church. So, if you're heading in that direction, think again. She isn't your type."

"Every pretty girl is my type, and she's the prettiest one I've seen here yet. I bet she's smart, too."

"Yeah. She and Greg Johnson are always at the top of the class."

"Well, old Charlie Thornton will be right up there with them this year."

I didn't comment. If I passed I wasn't unhappy. At least until I got my report card home. Mom and Dad both have the idea I should be turning those Cs and Ds into As and Bs. But they don't complain as much now as they used to. I think they've finally decided that maybe I'm not the same as my brothers and sisters. I don't know why it took them so long. I've been getting those Cs and Ds since back in elementary school.

Anyway, we got home and Charlie said we'd go downtown after lunch and pick up our pens and such. That was fine with me, though to tell the truth I'd always let Mom take care of it in the past. I was apt to forget half the things I needed and then blow the rest of the money on pool.

But Mom said it was okay for me to go with Charlie. I guess she figured he'd see that I got the right stuff.

He did. He'd made notes of what each teacher had said, and then he'd made a neat list of everything he needed. We stopped first at the bank so I could take some money out of my account and pay him back the forty he'd given me Friday night.

After that, we went to the drugstore and whatever he got, I got, too. We managed fine.

We met a group of about five girls including Sophie and Ava, and all of us went to Harry's Restaurant and killed about an hour goofing around before Harry kicked us out. He's always kicking us out, so it was no big deal. We dropped off a couple of girls, and then went home.

Mom was pleased to see how well I'd managed. She said she sure was glad Charlie had moved here.

After dinner, Luke called. "A bunch of us are going down to the school to play football. You want to come?"

"I looked for you after school, but you were gone."

"Jamie needed help getting some stuff ready for the cheerleaders. They're holding tryouts next week."

"Oh. Where is she now? Isn't she going to play football with us?"

"Don't act dumb. She had some things to do at home. She said it wouldn't hurt for me to start getting ready for football season. So—are you coming or not?"

"Yeah, I guess. I'll see if Charlie wants to come, too."

"You think he'd take a chance on messing up that pretty face?"

"Yeah, right."

"The guy looks—well, like a creep. That smile—it's like he pastes it on in the morning and keeps it there all day. You know what he reminds me of? A plastic mannequin from a store window. It's a wonder he can move."

"He played baseball okay, didn't he?"

"Give me a break, Glen. Like that was a serious game! Or didn't you realize we had girls playing who didn't know a double play from a bunt?"

"I still think I should ask him to come. After all, he's new here and just getting to know people."

Luke snorted. "Getting to know people? Don't you mean getting to know girls? And he seems to be doing okay from what I saw."

"Well, this would give him a chance to know some guys, too."

"Bring him along if you have to. I don't care. Just make sure he knows it's football we're playing, not hopscotch."

Charlie was eager to go, so we drove to the school parking lot and walked over to the football field. He examined it closely and told me he was surprised at how good it was.

About ten minutes after we arrived, Luke and the others appeared. Soon there were enough guys for a good work-out. Charlie and Brandon and I were on one team; Luke and Matt on the other. As usual, Luke was quarterback for his team. About fifteen minutes in, we were getting bombed, so Charlie offered to take over as quarterback for our side. Man, was he hot! I forget the final score, but it was pretty lopsided in our favor.

Afterward, Luke didn't say much, but the rest of the guys were all excited over Charlie's playing. They figured that with him calling the plays the school team would be unbeatable this year.

Charlie took it pretty well. He just said we'd have to see what the coach thought about his playing first, and maybe somebody else would be better.

I went over to Luke, who stood a little apart from the crowd around Charlie. "Looks like maybe he does know how to play a little," I said.

Luke took the time to glare at me before he picked up his football and walked toward his car.

Charlie and I dropped in at The Peabody Diner later, but there wasn't much happening, so we drove around town and I pointed out where the Grants live. Charlie parked across the street and we read the sign on the church next door: Wallace Community Evangelical Church. It was a fairly small building, but new and not bad looking. The Grants' house was new, too—a bungalow similar to mine.

Charlie wanted to know more about the Grant family, so I told him there was a mother, a father, a brother— Paul—in his second year of high school, and two younger sisters in elementary school. You could see Charlie's brain working, figuring all the angles. I felt sure he was enjoying it, too. He was like a general planning his campaign strategy.

So far, every girl he'd met had fallen all over herself being nice to him. That included Jamie, although she hadn't been as obvious as some of the others. Nicole hadn't even spoken to Charlie this morning, except to say, "Hi," after he said it first. She showed no interest in him at all. So now Charlie was ready to do battle. Like he'd said, every pretty girl was his type, and he wanted Nicole to know it.

The campaign began at school the next day. We were barely inside the building when we saw Nicole and Zoey at their lockers just outside our homeroom.

Charlie, a perfect gentleman, offered to carry Nicole's books. She gave him a little smile, then said, "Thanks, but I can manage."

"Your name is Nicole, isn't it? I like that. Did you know it means 'victorious one'?"

She smiled but turned to Zoey. "Come on, or we'll be late for homeroom."

I remembered that our teacher was Mr. Jackman. "Yeah, come on, Charlie. We don't want to be late."

Charlie was staring at Nicole's back, but when I spoke he quickly organized his books and shut his locker.

Morning classes weren't bad. I guess school is usually fun for a couple of days. After that it's downhill all the way.

Nicole and Zoey were with a group of other girls during lunch, so Charlie didn't get a chance to talk to Nicole. He was stuck with trying to extricate himself from Sophie, Ava, Marta, and several other girls who all wanted to sit with him. Luke was with Jamie. He even carried her tray over to the table and went back to get his own. Man, but she had him hooked.

I sat with Matt and Brandon and we watched Charlie. He was pretty smooth. He talked to all of the girls by turns, not singling out any of them, but apparently keeping them all interested. It made me tired just to watch. I was glad when it was time for phys ed.

When the last bell rang, we were stuck in shop, so Charlie had to hurry to get to Nicole's locker before she left.

I tried to hide my grin as I followed along behind. Life certainly was getting more interesting.

"Hey, Nicole," Charlie called, "wait up!"

She was just shutting her locker. When he called, she paused and looked back. She shifted her books from one arm to the other and waited.

"Just wanted to ask if you'd like a ride home. I've got my car here today. You look like you've got a lot of books."

She laughed. "Oh, not too many. Thanks for the offer, but no thanks."

She walked off with Zoey.

Charlie stood watching them for a moment. Then he turned to me. "Well, come on. What are you waiting for?"

We drove home without talking. I knew Charlie's mind was in a whirl. Nicole had to be the only girl in the school who would turn down a ride in his car.

Charlie had no more luck the next day. He asked Nicole to go for a Coke after school, and she said she had to go straight home. When he offered to drive her home, she politely said, "No, thank you."

The following day he got sidetracked with tryouts for the football team. As I'd expected, after the coach saw him throw and run, he was a shoo-in for quarterback.

Luke was pretty upset. Not that it was obvious, but Luke and I have been pals for quite a while, so I know the signs. He'd assumed, before Charlie came, that he was the logical choice for quarterback, but he was no match for Charlie.

Charlie had dragged me out to the tryouts with him. I did my best, but when the coach asked me if I'd like to be the team manager, I knew what that meant—looking after uniforms, finding lost gear, fetching water, and whatever random jobs came up.

I said, "No, thanks, Mr. Wilton. I didn't really want to be on the team, anyway."

I guess it sounded like sour grapes, but it was actually the truth. I *didn't* want to be on the team. Oh, I don't mind doing some punting and catching for an hour or two, or even having a scrimmage now and then, but I don't need those practices at seven in the morning or after school. Nor do I need to try to remember patterns and numbers and positions and all that stuff. Not to mention getting the broken arms and the sprained ankles and assorted other injuries that I've noticed are an all-too-frequent part of the game. I'd tried out because Charlie wanted me to, but I was whistling when I went home to see if Mom had baked any cookies that day. Friday is her day for baking.

And yeah, I know having a stay-at-home Mom who loves to cook is pretty rare these days. I so appreciate it!

That night, Charlie was pretty high, what with being named quarterback and his dad's having given him an extra hundred bucks for making him proud or something. I'd like to see my dad just hand me a hundred bucks!

Oh, well, some of us have it made, and some of us have to keep struggling on.

We blew a good deal of the money at the diner. Charlie found some girls and a few guys joined in, and I guess we made a lot of noise. When we got kicked out, Peggy—a blonde with big blues eyes and a well-developed figure—said her mom wouldn't mind if we went to her house, and by the time the word passed around, about twelve of us ended up going there. Peggy's mom didn't seem too concerned—she just set out lemonade and chips and left the room.

Somebody put some music on and there was a ready-made dance. Fortunately, there were a couple more guys than girls, so I was able to act as DJ, and sit back and watch without anybody saying a word. We left around midnight.

I had to work Saturday morning. Dad had asked me to trim our bushes and trees, and I knew several neighbours who'd pay me to trim theirs. So I was up at seven and worked until eight at night. I made a hundred and forty dollars. Not a bad day's work.

Mom said Charlie had called while I was out, so I wandered over to his house and knocked on the door. His dad answered. I hadn't seen him before, but you couldn't mistake him. He was just an older version of Charlie—same build, same colour hair, same grin. He had a half-empty glass in his hand and he was laughing about something. When he saw me, he said, "Well, hey, you must be Glen! Charlie's told me about you. Sure nice of you to take him under your wing and show him around. Sorry he's not here right now though. Some girl called him and he took off. Don't know when he'll be back."

I said thanks and went home. I'd worked pretty hard all day, so what I really wanted was to have a shower and go to bed. I was glad Charlie had found something to do.

Sunday morning, I got the shock of my life. I was still asleep when Mom knocked on my door and came in to say that Charlie was there with a suit on and he wanted to see me.

Now, Sunday is normally my day for sleeping in. But I got up and put on my robe and went out to the living room. Sure enough, there was Charlie in a dark blue suit with a tie and all. I guess I looked kind of dazed because he laughed.

Then he said, "Come on. Grab some clothes. Don't you know this is Sunday morning?"

"Huh?"

"Sunday morning. Where do people go on Sunday morning?"

"How should I know?"

"They go to church, man. Like to the Wallace Community Evangelical Church."

Chapter 4

My mind cleared a little. I vaguely remembered going to a Sunday school when I was a kid. But it had been a long time ago. "Church doesn't start till eleven."

"Not this one. Church is at ten. There's something called The Learning Center after."

A bit dazed, I went back to my room. I rummaged around and finally found the suit I'd had to get for my sister Jeanne's wedding in the spring. I got dressed. Charlie came in to hurry me up and I made him look for my tie. Why I was going with him I didn't know, unless maybe because I wanted to see Nicole's reaction when she saw Charlie at church. Yeah, who'd want to miss that?

As I followed Charlie out the front door, I yelled to Mom that we were going to church.

I think she yelled back, "You're what?" but I didn't stop to answer.

Charlie told me to reach in his glove compartment for a food bar. Sure enough, he had some kind of bar that was equivalent to a good breakfast. So I ate one. He said he kept a couple on hand just in case. Charlie seemed to think of everything.

We made it to the church with seconds to spare. A man wearing a badge that said "usher" asked us if we needed a bulletin and gave us a folded paper. He showed us to some seats halfway down the side. There weren't any hard pews, just comfortable brown cloth chairs.

We'd barely sat down when Nicole's dad—they called him Pastor Grant—got up to announce we were going to sing a song, and words came up on a screen behind him. Church was on.

During the singing, I glanced around a bit. Nicole was on the other side near the front, sitting with her mother and two younger sisters. Her brother Paul was with some of his friends closer to the back.

I also saw a guy from our class—Ted Bradden. He was with two other guys I knew—Andy Parker, who was in grade eleven, and Derek Palmer, who was in one of the other grade twelve classes. These were the guys Nicole was friendly with. They were all sitting together a couple of rows from the back on the side Charlie and I were on. None of them were wearing suits. I also saw Zoey, sitting almost directly across from Charlie and me with her mom and sister.

The song ended, and we sat down before singing another. As I might have guessed, Charlie was a pretty good singer. Personally, I'm tone deaf. At least, I've been told that any note I try to sing ends up sounding just like any other note I try to sing. Fortunately, there's hardly ever any need for anyone to hear me. Now I just kind of mumbled the words. Charlie drowned me out, anyway.

The church service kept going. Some lady sang—pretty well, it seemed to me—and then there was a prayer and the offering. Charlie had thought to bring some money, but he hadn't reminded me.

Next came another song and another prayer and all the little kids went out. Then came what they called the sermon, which seemed to last a long time. I don't really remember anything about it because the whole time I was wondering if Nicole would be friendlier to Charlie now that he'd come to her church, or if she just didn't like him. I had a lot of trouble believing that.

Finally, there was another song, and after that the service was over. I thought Charlie would try to talk to Nicole, but he didn't. We walked toward the back where Pastor Grant stood. People were shaking hands with him, so Charlie did, too.

"I really enjoyed the sermon," Charlie said. "Especially the part about Moses' crossing the Red Sea. What you said about all of us having challenges in our lives, that's so true. I guess mine is moving to a new town and having to make all new friends. And finding a church, too."

"Well, we're certainly glad to have you visit with us," Pastor Grant said. He wanted to know Charlie's name, and who I was, and on and on. Pastor Grant said we would certainly be welcome here.

The next thing I knew he was telling Charlie about a group for young people and how it met in a room downstairs and how we were welcome to attend.

I signalled to Charlie that I'd just as soon get out of there, but I knew it was hopeless. Naturally, he wanted to stay. It would make a good impression on you-know-who.

Somebody named Mr. Reiss came up and said he was the youth leader, so there wasn't much I could do but meekly follow him and Charlie down the stairs.

There were about eight or nine of us in the little back room. We sat on those stacking chairs that are okay to sit on for about twenty minutes. Mr. Reiss started by praying that we would all learn something useful, and then he began talking about somebody called Paul who was in prison singing. If I was included in his prayer about us learning something, I guess his prayer didn't work.

Charlie paid attention, though, and he even answered a few questions. Mr. Reiss seemed pleased, but it was hard to tell about Nicole. She didn't seem any friendlier to Charlie than she'd been at school.

When it was over, the girls left right away but Charlie stayed around and talked to the guys and Mr. Reiss. I wasn't paying too much attention, so when Charlie came over and said he was ready to go, I almost jumped. Truth was I'd missed some sleep that morning, thanks to Charlie, and I was awfully close to making it up.

In the car, Charlie was really happy. He figured his strategy had paid off and Nicole would be a lot friendlier the next day. I said that I hoped so, because then he wouldn't think he had to drag me to church with him every week. He just laughed.

But he wasn't laughing the next day. He cornered Nicole and asked her to go for a Coke with him after school. She said she was busy.

"Oh? What are you doing that's so important?"

She didn't look at him. "I have to go home right after school."

"It doesn't take that long to have a Coke, you know."

"I have to work on my report for English class."

"That isn't due until Wednesday."

"Well, I want to get it done today."

"You can afford half an hour for a Coke. All work and no play makes Jane a dull girl. I wouldn't want you to get dull."

She was looking past him at the lockers. "I'm sorry. I just can't." She started to go, but Charlie stood in her way.

"What is this? I'm beginning to think you don't want to go out with me. Don't you want to go alone? Well, Glen can come, too. Why don't you ask your friend Zoey?"

"I'm sorry. I really *am* in a hurry to get home." This time she pushed past him.

Charlie just stared after her.

I walked up to him.

"Did you see that?" he said without looking at me.

"Yeah."

"I don't believe it. You'd think she didn't like me or something."

"Yeah."

"But that's ridiculous!"

"Yeah. Let's go." I started down the corridor and Charlie followed. I guess he'd had a bit of a shock or something. I wondered what he'd do next. I didn't see him giving up easily.

After school Thursday, I walked with Charlie to football practice. All he could talk about was the upcoming game against the Riverside Rattlers. He was working out strategy with the coach, and he was as happy as could be. Apparently, girls didn't enter the picture. He wanted me to stay and watch, or maybe see if the coach didn't still want me to manage. I had nothing else to do, so I said I'd watch. But that was it.

It was kind of interesting to be able to sit back and observe. For one thing, I saw that Charlie pretty well took charge of the practice. Even the coach asked him what he thought and used his ideas. I guess he had what you call leadership ability as well as plain football ability. He had it made.

Except with Luke. Luke was in as wide receiver, and although he seemed to be catching the ball when Charlie threw it his way, I caught a couple of the looks he gave Charlie's back when no one was looking. Charlie was positively not at the top of Luke's People to Make Friends With list.

I had my books with me, so I figured I may as well get them out and take care of some homework. I did get a few algebra problems more or less done before I dozed off. I woke up to find Charlie standing in front of me laughing.

"Were we so bad that we put you to sleep?"

I picked up a book that had fallen. "Not you. My algebra."

"Well, did you stay awake long enough to see the team?"

"Yeah." I stood up and we started walking. "You seemed to be doing okay."

"Okay? Is that all you can say? Riverside is going to have to be some team to even get on the scoreboard against us!"

"If you say so."

Charlie took a fake swing at me.

"Okay, I'll have to admit you looked pretty good. I doubt very much if Riverside will have a chance."

"That's better."

We walked on in silence for a while. Charlie shifted his books to his other arm and turned to look at me. "Hey, today's Thursday, right?"

"Yeah."

"Weekend starts tomorrow and we haven't made any plans."

"You've got a football game Saturday afternoon."

"Yeah. Hey, didn't I hear something about a dance at the school Saturday night?"

"You could have."

"Okay, Saturday game and dance. What should we do tomorrow night?"

"You've got football practice after school."

"Hey, didn't Mr. What's-his-name say something about a party Friday night? Sure he did. Man, I wish I could remember what he said."

"What on earth are you talking about?"

"You know. At church. Or rather, in that group afterwards. What's his name? Oh, yeah, Reiss. He said something about Friday."

"I never heard him say anything about it. Even if he did, I'm not interested."

"Oh, come on, Glen, where's your curiosity? Don't you want to see what Nicole and her friends do instead of going to movies and dances like us normal people?"

"Not really."

"Come on, it'll be good for laughs. Anyway, it'll score some points with Nicole."

"Maybe."

"You don't sound very excited."

"Why should I be? You're the one that wants to score the points, not me."

"Okay. That's true." Charlie sounded hurt. "I guess it was selfish of me to expect you to come along just to keep me company."

I was immediately sorry I'd sounded so childish. "Hey, I didn't mean anything! Just ignore me when I get grumpy. Everyone else does."

Charlie grinned. "Then you'll come with me to the youth thing?"

"Yeah, sure, I guess. But we don't know what time or anything."

"So I'll ask Nicole."

Sure enough, right after lunch the next day, Charlie walked up to Zoey and Nicole, who were talking outside the school's front doors.

"Hi, girls. Isn't it a terrific day? You coming to the football game tomorrow afternoon?"

They stopped talking and looked at Charlie. Zoey answered. "Probably. Are you playing?"

I was a few steps behind Charlie. "Is he playing? More like starring. He's quarterback."

Zoey gave me a puzzled look. "Is that good?"

Nicole laughed. "Zoey, you'd better stick to checkers."

Charlie flashed his big smile. "Hey, that reminds me. There's a youth meeting tonight, isn't there? Glen and I are planning to come, but neither of us remembered to write down the time and place."

Nicole and Zoey both looked at me in surprise.

I decided my shoelaces needed to be retied.

After what felt like a really long pause, Nicole answered. "It's at eight o'clock, at my house. We'll be playing games, singing, and having a devotional. Are you sure you and Glen are interested in coming?"

"Of course, we are. Right, Glen?"

I wanted to say I was about as interested in going to the youth meeting as I was in climbing the Himalayas, but my mother's efforts to instill good manners in me paid off. I contented myself with a nod.

"Do you need a ride, Zoey?" were Charlie's next words. Boy, he was prepared to do anything to get into Nicole's favor!

Zoey said no, she had a ride.

Then the bell rang, and we had to go in to class.

After school, Charlie had football practice, so I went down to Harry's with Matt and Brandon for some root beer, and then over to Ed's Pool Hall. No need to mention who lost. Finally, Brandon said it was time for them to hit the road, so I walked home. As I walked, I tried to think of an excuse for not going to the youth meeting with Charlie. But I didn't come up with anything I thought he'd believe.

I had no idea what to wear to a youth group party. I sure had no plans to wear a suit. At last, I dug out a pair of decent-looking jeans and the shirt I'd worn to the dance the week before.

Mom gave me a funny look when I came out, but she kept quiet.

Dad said, "That isn't Glen, is it? You know, the sloppy kid in a dirty T-shirt who never combs his hair?"

I ignored him. "I might be late. I'm not sure. Probably no later than midnight."

"Are you going with Charlie?" Mom asked.

"Yeah."

"That's good."

Let's face it, my mom thought Charlie was terrific. When I was with him, I made it on time for dinner, I changed my clothes now and then, and I didn't bother Dad for the car.

"Is it too much to ask where you're going?" Dad said.

"The Grants."

"Grants?"

"You know. Nicole's house."

"I didn't know you'd been to her house," Mom said.

"I haven't. Anyway, I'm just going with Charlie. There's some kind of party. We heard about it at church last week."

"Okay," Dad said, but I could tell he was puzzled.

"Can I go now?"

"I guess so. Need any money?"

I was so surprised I just stared at him.

"Glen?"

"Sorry, I thought you asked me if I needed money."

"I did." Dad was smiling now. "Is that so strange?"

"I thought I had to earn my money."

"You do. But I know most of your earnings are in the bank. I thought you might be short of spending money."

"No, I'm okay. I doubt if I'll need much tonight, anyway."

"You should buy some gas for Charlie's car since you ride in it so much."

"That's a good idea. I'll do it soon. Well, don't bother to wait up for me."

"Of course not," Mom said, lying without any hesitation. Every one of her kids grew up knowing she never went to sleep until they were in.

"Have a good time," Dad called as I went out the door. Imagine him asking if I needed money!

Charlie was getting his car out of the garage when I walked over. Both his parents' cars were gone.

If possible, Charlie looked shinier than I'd seen him yet. As usual, his clothes looked brand new. His hair was combed just right. He had on his biggest, flashiest smile.

We got to the Grants' a few minutes early. Other kids were going in. Charlie combed his hair even though he didn't need to. He handed me his comb, so I used it a bit. No doubt I needed it, but with my crazy hair, I doubt if it made much of a difference.

Charlie barely rang the doorbell before Nicole's brother Paul opened it. It may have been my imagination, but I think he gave me a funny look. But he said, "Hi," and showed us where to go downstairs.

The Grants have a really nice family room with a fireplace and lots of stuffed chairs. Most of the kids from church were already there, plus a few others. We found chairs and I sat back while Charlie talked to a couple of kids and more people arrived.

Then Mr. Reiss took charge and got everyone involved in games. Charlie found himself playing Scrabble with Jo-Ann Millar, Nicole, and Ted Bradden.

I wound up in a crokinole game. I've played it quite a bit at home, so I did okay.

After a reasonable time, we all had to switch, and I ended up as Nicole's partner in a game of Jeopardy. That wasn't much fun. I never was very good at that sort of game, and I guess I was worried about her having such a lousy partner. She was nice about it, of course, but I was sure glad when it was over.

Next we played charades. I did what the kids on my team told me to do, but mostly I just enjoyed watching. Charlie was in his element here, and Nicole was good, too. But it was Zoey who surprised me. She was really good! Not at all what I'd have expected, since she's so— well, insignificant—at school. Stands to reason, since she's on the plain side (as Mom would say) and doesn't seem to care very much about how she looks, and she's always with Nicole, who's a knock-out (as Charlie and any other guy with two eyes would say). But I guess Zoey has some strong points, too, and acting is certainly one of them.

By the time we finished charades, it was nearly ten o'clock. We gathered around the fireplace, and a couple of kids got out guitars, and everyone was given a little song book, and they started singing. I listened. Some of the kids knew how to sing harmony, and it was really nice. I don't think Charlie knew the songs, but he picked them up quickly, and he did just fine.

When the singing ended with a very soft, really smooth song, Mr. Reiss started talking. I was feeling a little sleepy, but I tried to listen to him. He was talking about what he called standards. Like in school there's a standard you have to meet in order to pass a grade. And to get a job you have to have the necessary skills. Then he got onto talking about God's standards and how it's impossible for anyone to meet them on his own. I think he said something about the passing grade to get into heaven being one hundred percent.

That's pretty high. If I get a sixty in school, I figure I'm doing great. Even if I worked as hard as my parents seem to think I could, I'd never get more than an eighty, or maybe a ninety if a miracle happened.

That's about all I got from his talk.

To be honest, I've never thought about heaven or God or anything like that. I went to a Sunday school a bit when I was little, but I figure I'm too old for that kind of stuff now. I wondered what all these other kids saw in it—especially Nicole, who has a lot of brains.

When the talk was over, somebody prayed and we quickly took care of several pizzas, soft drinks, and ice cream sundaes.

When people started leaving, Charlie and I joined them. But before we reached the door, Charlie went into the kitchen and thanked Mrs. Grant for letting us use her house and for making the food and all. She asked him where he was from and who his folks were and stuff like that. They were still talking when the last of the people went out the door.

I was leaning against a wall, trying not to attract attention. I could hear the conversation in the kitchen and I have to admit I was enjoying it. Until Paul and Nicole turned from saying good-bye to the last of their guests and saw me.

"Glen," Nicole said, "I didn't realize you were still here. Were you waiting for something?"

"Uh, Charlie."

They looked a little puzzled, but then Charlie's voice came from the kitchen, so they understood. The three of us stood there awkwardly.

Finally, Paul said, "What did you think of Mr. Reiss's talk?"

I swallowed hard. "Uh, it was okay, I guess." I looked toward the kitchen door. "Maybe I'll see if Charlie's coming."

Paul and Nicole followed me to the kitchen. As we went in, Charlie was explaining to Mrs. Grant how hard it had been to leave all his friends when he moved. He saw me and added, "Of course, having Glen across the street sure has helped. I don't know what I'd have done if he hadn't taken pity on me and showed me around."

Mrs. Grant gave me an approving smile. "I believe we've met before, Glen, but I haven't really talked to you. I'm glad you've been so helpful to Charlie. He's been telling me how hard it was to move. We'll all have to help him feel at home here in Wallace."

Fortunately, she turned to look at Paul and Nicole, so I was spared having to fumble for something to say. I gave Charlie what I hoped was a meaningful look indicating my desire to get out of the house. He smiled at me. Then, in his most polite voice, he said, "But it's getting late and I know you're wishing we'd get out of here, so we'll move on."

Mrs. Grant hastily said she had no such wish.

Charlie laughed. "Well, the truth is I should have been asleep ages ago. I have a football game tomorrow—the first game of the year—so I want to be sharp. Thanks again for a great evening."

We headed for the door and after a few more good-byes got onto the front step. We walked to the car and climbed inside. Charlie started the motor and pulled out. Then he looked over at me and winked. "Well," he said with satisfaction, "was I hot or was I hot?"

I laughed. "Yeah, I guess you were all right."

"'Always get on the good side of a girl's mother' is strategy number one. Remember that. Of, course, that's only if the girl is playing hard to get. Or if you want to impress her with your maturity."

I just looked at him. Since I'd never been in the position of trying to make a girl like me, I guess maybe I lacked some of the appreciation I should have felt. On the other hand, it was sure fun watching Charlie at work, and listening to him butter up Mrs. Grant had been hilarious.

"So what's next?" I asked.

"Well, I'm going to get Nicole to go out with me, of course. I just have to think of something she can't refuse. I know she's just playing the game. She knows that a girl who's easy to get will also be easy to get rid of. So she's going to make me work. That's okay. I appreciate the challenge. But now," he said as we turned the corner toward the diner, "how about a little action of a different kind?"

Chapter 5

I didn't say anything. We were already pulling into a parking space. Charlie said he wanted a drink.

I was stuffed from the party, so I didn't get anything.

In a couple of minutes, Charlie came back with Ava. "Sophie's sick, so Ava came over with some other girls. I said we'd give her a ride home."

I got into the back so Ava could sit up front with Charlie. This time there was no need to pretend she was interested in me; it was quite apparent that she thought Charlie was Mr. Wonderful. He didn't discourage her thoughts.

I really had to admire him. Maybe I wasn't interested in girls myself, but it sure was an education watching how easily Charlie managed to make girls think he was crazy about them.

The only thing was that I wasn't sure what he'd do differently if ever it was for real. But I guess he'd know.

Anyway, he and Ava talked and giggled and ate, and then he drove around for a bit before he took her home. I waited in the car for quite a while before he came back from walking her to her door.

He was grinning. "Not a bad night, eh?"

"Nope," I agreed.

"If only Ava looked like Nicole," he mused.

"Or if Nicole acted like Ava," I replied.

"Yeah." He whistled.

"Of course, then Nicole wouldn't be Nicole and Ava wouldn't be Ava," I said.

He laughed. "Let's not get hung up on philosophy. Anyway, I'm going to make Nicole act like Ava. You just wait and see."

I grinned. "We'll see."

"You don't believe me? Want to place a small wager? Or maybe a big one?"

"No bets. I always lose. Anyway, I don't really care. I mean, it's fun either way."

He grinned. "I ought to charge you a fee for front row seats. You seem to feel this is some kind of show just for your viewing pleasure."

"Well, it is kind of fun to watch."

"Yeah, well you keep watching. Because Nicole Grant is going to be my girl, and that's that!"

My dad had lined up a job for me doing some fall clean-up work for Mrs. Pearson, an elderly neighbour of ours who can't do that sort of thing herself. Painting a fence and splitting up perennials isn't really my idea of something to do on a Saturday morning, but she paid well, so it wasn't all bad.

In the afternoon, I went to the game with Matt and Brandon. With Charlie at quarterback and Luke catching like he had glue on his fingers and running like someone under fire, we took an early lead and were never seriously challenged. The score was 45-24 for us.

That night, Charlie and I went to the school gym for the dance. We were barely through the front doors before he was swamped with both girls and guys who wanted to tell him how wonderful he was.

Luke and Jamie came in right behind us, and a few kids went over to talk to them, but the majority stayed with Charlie. A couple of people called over something like, "You were great, too, Luke."

I went over to Luke. "Good game today."

"Yeah? Nice of you to notice."

Jamie had her arm linked through Luke's, but she moved away a bit and looked at him. "You don't need to be jealous," she said. "Charlie can't help being good. Everybody's just glad to have him here. They already knew you'd be good, but they didn't expect to have him, too. We've got an excellent chance of winning it all this year."

"Yeah?" Luke wasn't mollified. "You seemed to be having a good time yelling for him this afternoon. 'Go, Charlie!' That's all I heard."

"The cheerleaders yelled for everyone. Of course we had to yell for the quarterback a lot. We also yelled, 'Go, Luke!' whenever you had the ball."

"Yeah? I guess I couldn't hear you under my helmet."

Jamie laughed. "You're so cute when you're mad."

"Well, keep talking about Charlie and you'll find out how cute I can get."

"Nope. I didn't come to a dance to talk about Charlie. Let's go work off your anger with some good exercise." She pulled on his arm.

"Exercise?" he said. "You think I want to dance with you to get some exercise?"

"Come on or I'll find somebody who *does* want to dance with me." Her voice was teasing as she pulled him down the hall toward the gym. "Like maybe Charlie." She let go of his arm and ran toward the gym door.

"You little—" Luke followed her.

Charlie had about six girls surrounding him as he also made his way toward the gym. He flashed me a grin and I gave him a thumbs-up signal. He too disappeared. I wondered how he'd choose one girl to dance with without annoying the others.

"So, Glen, how's it going?" I'd thought I was alone in the hallway, but Marta was standing behind me, near my left side.

I turned to look at her. "Uh, it's, uh, going fine."

"How come *you* don't play football?" she asked, her head tilted back as if examining me. She had on a shiny black shirt and a short black leather skirt with black tights. With her long straight black hair and black lipstick and nail polish, I couldn't help thinking that all she needed was a broom and a pointy hat and she'd be totally ready for Halloween.

But all I said was, "You know I don't play football."

"I heard you tried out, but when they told you to run left and you ran right, the coach decided to make you water boy. Only you couldn't find the water cooler, so he fired you from that, too."

"Sure, Marta, whatever you say."

"So how come Charlie spends so much time with you? Unless maybe it's because you're such complete opposites it's like one of those magnetic things. You know, positive and negative attraction."

My immediate thought was how Nicole had all the positives and Marta all the negatives. But all I said was, "I think you're getting confused with electrons and protons."

"No, Glen, you're more like the neutron."

"If that's true, why are you wasting your time talking to me?"

"Good question. I guess I needed something to bring me down to earth after the excitement of talking to Charlie. But you've done the job." She walked past me into the gym.

I followed along after a minute. The gym was decorated in the school colours, with lots of streamers and balloons and football banners on the walls. There was a band from Stanton on the stage, and a number of people dancing throughout the gym. Luke was dancing with Jamie. What else is new? Charlie was with Sophie.

There were some chairs and a few tables along the near side. Matt and Brandon were sitting with a few other guys. I found a chair and rehashed the game with the guys.

Charlie came over a few times, but mostly he danced with one girl after another. He ended up dancing the last dance with Marta and offering to take her home. He expected me to tag along, but I preferred to stay out of Marta's line of fire. She'd likely talk about me behind my back, but I didn't mind that. It was the conversation *with* me I couldn't take. So I walked. The night was clear and warm and it was no problem.

Sunday morning Charlie showed up about nine-thirty in a good pair of pants and a shirt, and more or less dragged me off to church with him. He said I could sleep through the sermon if I wanted, but we were going. Mom and Dad looked pretty amused as he shoved me out the front door.

I actually did come very close to sleeping through the sermon. Charlie nudged me now and then, and that kept me from fading right out.

In the youth group afterwards, I had to kind of sit up and not look too much like an idiot. I kept wondering what I'd say if anyone asked me a question—like what was I doing there?

Somehow, I lived through it. But I had no idea if our being there was having any effect on Nicole. If it was, she certainly didn't let on. She spoke to Charlie only when he spoke first, and then she said only what was absolutely necessary. But Charlie remained confident that he was gaining ground.

During the week, he asked her out twice and she turned him down both times. He told me she was just playing hard to get, and he'd wait till she was ready. Anyway, he didn't have a lot of time to waste thinking about her. This was football season.

In English class Thursday we got something else to think about. Each year, the senior class puts on a play in the late fall. It's kind of a tradition. This year, the chosen play was *The Importance of Being Earnest*. I didn't know anything about it, but Charlie said it was okay.

A list was passed and you had to sign up for something. There were two male and two female parts that were supposed to be pretty good, and then a few others. I wasn't at all surprised to see Charlie sign up for one of the male leads. What did surprise me was to see Luke sign his name under Charlie's. The idiot! Why didn't he try out for the other male lead?

Marta had her name down for one of the female leads. Nicole didn't. She had hers under Lady something who was the mother of one of the female leads. That was maybe kind of strange, because I knew Nicole was a good actress. Or was this a way to avoid Charlie?

Charlie wanted me to try for the part of some preacher. He thought that would be funny. I didn't. Finally, I said I'd help with props. Things like moving tables and stuff I understand.

Charlie had noticed Luke was trying out for the same part he was (Algernon something), and he thought that was great. Apparently, he'd done quite a bit of acting and figured he was as good as in the part already. He denied it, but all the same he seemed to relish the thought of beating out Luke again. I didn't say much.

After school, while Charlie had football practice, I went home. Mom was in the kitchen baking bread.

I got some milk and cookies and then said, "Mom, why do you think Luke would deliberately try out for the same part as Charlie when there's another part just as good?"

"What are you talking about?"

So I had to explain about the play and all. She thought Luke might have a chance to get the part. I didn't.

But she was more concerned over what I was doing. "Why don't *you* try out for the other part?"

"Me act in the play? You have to be kidding!"

"Why not? You could do it if you wanted. You just don't want to have the work of memorizing."

"Mom, you must be confusing me with one of your other children. I can't act!"

"And when have you ever tried?"

I started to remind her of the time I fell off the stage while playing the part of a tree in third grade, but she didn't give me a chance.

"Glen Sauten, I'm tired of hearing you say you're not good at anything! I think it's a cop-out! I think you could act just as well as Luke or Charlie, but we'll never know because you won't even try!"

I shoved a cookie in my mouth and waited to see if the storm was over. Mom rarely yells at me. Or anyone.

She got the bread out of the oven and then said, "I'm sorry. Glen. But sometimes I do wish you'd maybe just try a few more new things. And not be quite so easy-going. But I still love you. And it's your decision." She gave me a hug and a few minutes later I heard her vacuuming in the living room.

I escaped to my room and sat there thinking about what she'd said. I decided mom must not be feeling well or something. I also decided it was a little late for me to change my personality.

In the game that Saturday, our team won by a wide margin. In addition to the cheerleaders, a lot of girls in the stands, and even some guys, were yelling, "Charlie! Charlie!" After the game they all made a big fuss over him again. Nicole wasn't one of them, although she'd been at the game with Zoey and Darlene.

Yeah, Luke got some attention, too. But nowhere near as much as Charlie.

Saturday night, Charlie and I cruised around for a while. There wasn't much going on. Finally, we found Marta with Emily, and Emily invited us back to her place for popcorn.

I wasn't anxious to be around Marta, and having been in the car that one afternoon with Emily, I knew she was a total flake, so I grimaced when Charlie looked at me. But I guess he was bored or something, because he agreed.

So we followed Marta's car to Main Street, where Emily lives in an apartment above the jewelry store.

Emily's mother seemed to be in bed, but she didn't mind our making popcorn and finding drinks and putting on some music. After a few minutes, Marta and Charlie got up and started dancing.

I tried to keep eating popcorn and avoid looking at Emily. She was eating popcorn, too, and spilling some of it. I stooped to pick up what she'd dropped. Unfortunately, that caused her to notice me.

She giggled. "I'm such a slob," she said. "But I dance pretty good."

"I don't." I said as I straightened up.

She giggled again and put down her drink. "Then I'll have to teach you," she said. She held out her hands and I pretty well had to take them.

So I danced with her. I'm not very good—partly because I don't have much of a sense of rhythm and partly due to lack of practice. But when I stepped on her toes she giggled and when she stepped on mine, she yelled, "Oops!" and giggled some more; so we managed.

After a while, Emily said, "Charlie, it's my turn to dance with you. Marta can't have you to herself all the time."

So I was forced to dance with Marta.

She wasn't any happier than I was, but since she put on fast music and continued talking to Charlie instead of me, it wasn't as bad as it might have been. I never had to actually touch her. She managed to get Charlie back after only one dance.

After that, I convinced Emily I needed to sit down, and we ate popcorn for as long as I could get away with it. I vowed silently to myself never to get caught in a situation like this again. Even going to church was better than this.

That thought led to an idea. At about eleven, I looked at my watch and said, "Well, I have to be up early for church tomorrow."

Marta and Emily just looked at me, but I could tell Charlie was having a lot of trouble keeping a straight face. He said he'd have to take me home, and we got out before the girls had time to argue.

Outside, Charlie leaned against the car, doubled up in laughter.

"It's not that funny," I said.

"Are you kidding? I've never seen anything so funny in my life. You said it with such honesty!" He laughed some more. "I have the strangest feeling you don't care for Emily and Marta."

"Now where did you ever get that idea?"

Charlie opened the passenger door. "Well, come on, Glen. We have to get you to bed early so you won't sleep through church again."

I actually did stay awake through the service the next morning. Pastor Grant talked about some guy he called the rich young ruler. It seemed this guy was really loaded with money and everything, but he'd made having a lot of money his priority and ignored other, more important things, like kindness to others. Pastor Grant asked if we had ever put the wrong things first in our lives. Obeying God was involved there, too, but I wasn't sure exactly how.

In the youth class, Mr. Reiss talked about what he called false gods. He said there's only one real God, but that lots of people have other gods instead of him—like money or power or other things like that. It occurred to me that Charlie was putting Nicole pretty high on his list.

Speaking of Nicole, she was wearing a top I'd never seen before. It was kind of soft, and it was a light shade of green. It looked really nice on her.

After the regular stuff was over, somebody mentioned Halloween and how there was going to be a youth party, and they wondered about using somebody's farmhouse again. Charlie got interested and before long he was in the middle of the discussion.

I was sitting by myself, waiting, when I noticed Nicole standing nearby reading a poster on the wall. When she turned and saw me staring at her, I quickly looked down at the floor. She came over.

"How'd you do on the math test, Glen?" she asked.

I shrugged. "Okay."

Silence.

I said, "How did you do?"

"Oh, fine."

"Charlie got ninety-five."

"I got ninety-seven."

"Oh." A pause. "Pretty good." I'd managed a whopping sixty-two.

More silence.

She tried again. "How do you like Mr. Reiss?"

"Oh, he's okay, I guess."

"Most of the kids think he's really good."

"Uh, sure. Real good." I looked around to see what Charlie was doing, but he was still talking. Grasping for words, I astutely said, "I guess they're planning something for Halloween."

"I guess so." Nicole didn't seem very interested.

"Did you have something last year?"

"Yes. Some people in the church have a farmhouse no one lives in, so we use it. We can have a campfire there, too, so it's kind of nice."

I nodded and searched in vain for something else to say. I wanted her to stop being polite and go talk to the other kids about the party.

"Well, I guess I'll go see if Mom's ready to leave."

I sighed with relief as I watched her go.

A few minutes later, the group broke up and Charlie seemed to be ready to go. But upstairs we found ourselves cornered by Mrs. Grant, who wanted to know if we'd like to come for lunch the next Sunday. Before I could get over my surprise, Charlie had said we'd be delighted to come if it wasn't too much trouble, and she'd said, "Of course it's no trouble."

We were outside before I thought of anything to say. "Charlie Thornton, I don't want to go to the Grants' house for lunch next Sunday! You can go. Tell them I've got the flu or the measles or something, but I'm not going, and that's final!"

Charlie just laughed. "We're moving, man. It won't be long now."

"You're crazy!"

"Not me. I'm about as savvy as they come."

"Oh, yeah, so why did Nicole get a higher mark on the math test?"

He stopped and stared at me. "Did she?"

"Ninety-seven."

He laughed. "Good for her! Beauty and brains. All she needs is the right guy to show her how to live."

"And that's you?"

"You know anybody better qualified?"

He had me there. Charlie was clearly all any girl could want. So why was Nicole still playing hard-to-get?

On Tuesday, Charlie asked Nicole to go to the Halloween party with him. She refused, saying she'd already been asked. Since the party was still a month away, Charlie had some cause for wondering if she was telling the truth.

The week dragged on. Our teachers seemed to be having some kind of competition to see who could give out the most work. Charlie and the others who were auditioning for the play were working on the scenes they'd been given. Props had nothing much to do yet, but we had one meeting to talk over what we would need to build for the sets.

That Friday, there was a youth meeting that apparently involved mostly studying the Bible. Since I not only didn't own a Bible but also figured I'd done enough for Charlie already, I was delighted to be able to tell him that I couldn't go. It was my dad's birthday, and my brothers and sisters were coming for the weekend.

Charlie went by himself and said it was pretty rough. The stuff they studied was all about dying, and he had to listen so he could ask questions to impress Nicole.

Meanwhile, I'd been playing Ping-Pong, eating birthday cake, listening to funny stories, and wrestling with the little kids. Poor Charlie.

Saturday, I messed around at home. Several family members had stayed over, so there was plenty to do. I didn't see much of Charlie because the football team had a game in another town.

But Sunday morning at nine, there was Charlie in our kitchen, telling Mom that I wouldn't be home early because of our having been invited out for dinner.

If looks could kill, Charlie'd have dropped on the spot, but they don't, and with Mom saying how nice it was of Mrs. Grant and all, there was nothing I could do to save myself.

Steaming mad, I sat beside Charlie through the church service and the youth group. Wouldn't you know it, Pastor Grant was talking about anger and how there are two kinds and what we should do about them and a bunch more stuff along that line!

If that wasn't enough, Mr. Reiss was into wisdom and how people who think they are wise are really foolish and how God can make the foolish wise. I decided I was neither wise nor foolish but halfway in between, and I didn't pay any more attention. Instead, I spent the time worrying about how I was going to live through the dinner coming up.

Mrs. Grant had set the table in the dining room. It looked nice. Since they have four kids and there were two of us, it was also pretty big. I wound up sitting between Paul and Charlie, which wasn't bad. Before dinner, I'd talked to one of the smaller girls.

All in all, it wasn't nearly as bad as I'd expected. The meal was good, and since Charlie was his usual talkative self, I could fade into the background. Twice, Mr. Grant asked me something, but both times it was fairly simple—did I work part-time and was I on a sports team, too? I said no each time.

When dinner was finished, Charlie insisted on helping Nicole and her mom clean up. I'd already planned my getaway. While Charlie was busy carrying some dishes to the kitchen, I found Mrs. Grant gathering more dishes in the dining room.

"Uh, thanks a lot for the dinner and all. Some of my family's in town, so I really have to get home. Thanks again for inviting me."

I was gone before Charlie came back from the kitchen. A little devious, maybe, but no more than Charlie had been in getting me there. I walked home feeling rather satisfied with myself. Charlie was where he wanted to be and I—I was where I wanted to be.

I learned on Monday that Charlie had spent the whole afternoon at the Grants' and gone to church with them again that night. Nicole had played Scrabble with him and talked to him quite a bit, and all in all he was pretty pleased with himself. He didn't say a word about my leaving the way I had. Everything seemed to be working out.

After lunch on Monday, Luke stopped me. Apparently Jamie was going away for the weekend, and since there was no football game, he actually had some time to himself.

I held back any sarcastic remarks I might have made.

He wanted to know if I'd still like to go camping down by Willard's Peak.

I didn't mind at all. For one thing, I'd be able to miss church. So I said sure, and we decided to ask Brandon and Matt.

Luke didn't mention Charlie, and neither did I.

But after school on Tuesday, I was standing near my locker with Charlie when Brandon came up. "Hey, Glen. I was just trying to figure out what I need to bring for the weekend. Food and stuff like that, I mean."

"You have plans for the weekend?" Charlie asked me.

"Uh, well, we, uh—we often spend a weekend in the summer at this place. Outdoors. We stay in tents."

"Yeah? Sounds interesting."

Brandon gave me a funny look and said, "I guess I'll talk to you later." Then he disappeared.

"So who all is going?" Charlie asked.

"Um, well, me and Luke and Brandon and Matt."

"Do you think you'd have room for one more? I've never camped outside before. We always stay at hotels. Should be fun. What do I need to bring?"

Chapter 6

I waited until Friday morning to tell Luke that Charlie was coming with us. I caught him going into the school with Jamie. "Uh, Luke. You got a minute?"

"Yeah, what? Is there a problem?"

"No. No problem. It's just—well, it seems Charlie found out about the weekend, and he's never been camping before and he asked if he could come and I said—I said he could."

Luke glared at me. "You what?"

"I said he could come."

"There isn't room."

"Sure there is. We've got two tents."

"He—he—"

"Live with it, Luke," said Jamie. "Besides, maybe if you two spend some time together, you'll discover you like each other. You do have a lot in common, you know."

"Yeah, like what? Besides him beating me out for quarterback, I mean?"

"Well, I hear he plays basketball, too."

Luke groaned.

"And girls like him," Jamie said sweetly.

Luke glared at her. "What girls?"

"Lots of girls."

"If you ever go near that creep—"

"Relax, Luke. You're much too tense." Jamie rubbed his back. "Stop worrying about Charlie. You need to treat him like an equal instead of a rival. This weekend will be good for you."

"You're responsible for him, Glen. The first time he screws up, that's it!"

I was willing to agree to anything.

Charlie had offered to take his car, but I didn't mention it to Luke. I told Charlie Luke's car was bigger and had more room for our gear, which was the truth. The fact that Luke's car is old and rusty green and more or less held together by paperclips I didn't go into. Long ago, we nicknamed his car the Goose, but I don't remember why. Maybe because when you drive with Luke you're sticking your neck out—you know, asking for trouble. You'll probably end up having to push.

Right after school, we hopped into Luke's car and drove around to pick up our gear. Then we headed north. Willard's Peak is about forty-five minutes away—just a nice drive. It's called a peak, but actually it's just a few hills that used to be mines.

At the bottom, on the east side of the hills, is this little creek surrounded by willows and rocks and just kind of perfect, if you know what I mean. It's the kind of place you could sit in for hours, just watching the birds and squirrels and kind of drinking in nature. Luke and I have been there quite a bit—before he took up with Jamie and forgot everything else. Anyway, it was nice to get back one more time.

We got our tents set up and made hot dogs over a fire. Charlie had somehow managed to pick up a case of beer, and that seemed to make Luke like him more. Brandon was kind of worried about having it, but Luke laughed at him and said there wouldn't be any cops bothering us out here. So we each had one or two and were feeling pretty good. I didn't drink much, myself. Really, none of us were that used to it, except maybe Charlie. At least, he talked as though he drank a lot.

Charlie had brought some cards, so we played poker. Luke won the first hand, and then Charlie won the second, and you could almost see the tension kind of building up between them. When Charlie started to deal the third hand, I got up. "I'm going for a walk," I replied to the questioning looks.

The others began playing, so I went alone. As I got further away, the sounds of their voices faded and I could hear the animals and birds around me. Water was lapping against the rocks on the near side of the creek. An owl was hooting on the other side, and there were oodles of crickets chirping. I heard the rustle of a field mouse or some small wood creature.

I sat down, listening to the sounds of nature and watching the ripple of the water as the sun went down. This was what I'd come for. The others could enjoy the weekend their way; I'd enjoy it mine.

I stayed there quite a while before I decided I should get back to the camp. I thought the others might have gone to bed. I was wrong.

I found Matt putting a bandage onto a cut above Charlie's eye. Brandon was in the tent looking after Luke.

Apparently, as Charlie kept winning at poker and both of them kept drinking, Luke got hotter and hotter. Finally, Luke accused Charlie of cheating, and took a swing at him. Luke caught Charlie by surprise and managed to connect with a solid right, but then Charlie picked himself up and knocked Luke down with an even harder punch. They were both okay, but, boy, they were going to have shiners tomorrow!

It was quite a while before our camp settled down. Charlie and I were in one tent and Brandon, Matt, and Luke in the other.

It was late the next morning before anyone got up. I was the only one who didn't have a headache. Brandon and Matt were basically okay, but both Charlie and Luke looked like they'd just spent a week in a jungle. They didn't feel so good, either.

Luke was embarrassed. Despite his fairly quick temper, he's not the kind of guy who goes around starting fist fights. I got him to apologize to Charlie, and Charlie said no hard feelings and they'd both had too much to drink, so a measure of peace was gained.

We sat around fishing most of the afternoon, and all of us had naps, so by dinner everyone felt pretty good. We managed to catch enough fish to make a meal, so we fried them, and Luke and I roasted corn and baked potatoes. My mom had sent two apple pies, so we pretty well stuffed ourselves.

After dinner, we cleaned up and went for a walk along the river bank. Charlie asked about the hills, so we told him how history has it that Abe Willard found silver there, and on his way to town to tell people, his horse stumbled, and Abe wound up a cripple, and how he lived in a little unpainted shack at the base of the hills and wouldn't accept help from anyone around; and how, after he was dead, folks found a couple of hundred thousand dollars worth of silver in his shack. And also how the rest of the silver was mined till it was gone, and now all that's left are two old mine shafts that are rotted and too dangerous to go in.

"Hasn't anyone been in them?" Charlie asked.

"Well," Brandon said, "one of them's so boarded up and overgrown that you'd have to be an ant to get in. Most of us have been inside the other one, but no more than a few steps."

"Could we climb over there tomorrow?" Charlie asked. "I've never been inside an old mine."

"Well," I said, "we could climb up to it, but it's really not safe to go inside."

"Yeah," Matt said. "There's all kinds of signs saying to stay out."

Charlie looked at Brandon. "I thought you said most of you had been inside."

"Well, you know. Just a quick look. It really isn't safe."

The next morning, Sunday, we were up fairly early. We caught a few fish and had a decent breakfast. After that, we hiked along the river until we found a place we could cross without getting soaked. After that, we climbed single file until we reached the first of the mines. This was the one that was impossible to get in. We looked at it for a minute and then went on to the second shaft. After about a ten-minute walk, we reached it. There were boards nailed across the opening, and signs that said DANGER! KEEP OUT! But as Brandon had said, all of us had been curious enough to find a way in at some time. It was a job of about twenty minutes to remove enough of the boards and brush to make an opening we could get through.

Luke went first. He'd brought a flashlight, so he turned it on and then eased himself in. Brandon and Matt followed. Charlie motioned for me to go ahead, so I did. He followed.

When we were all in, Luke used the flashlight to point out the things in the mine—the track the cars traveled on to carry the ore, some old rusty parts of discarded tools, a lantern, places where you could see someone had dug into the walls, though I suspect the diggings were more recent than the mine.

We walked a few steps, with Luke pointing things out. He seemed to be trying to impress Charlie.

Brandon said, "Hey, I think we've gone far enough."

"The mine looks pretty sturdy to me," Charlie said. "Still, if you're afraid—"

"He's not afraid," Luke said belligerently.

We walked in a bit farther, Luke leading and the rest of us following. Charlie stopped to examine something— what, I don't know, because it was too dark to see much at all.

Just then, Luke shouted, "Hey, what's this?" He pointed his light at a spot on the wall.

"It's shiny," Matt said as he and Brandon went over to see.

I looked around for Charlie, but in the dark I couldn't see him. I yelled, "Charlie, where are you?" just as Luke used a piece of rock he'd found to try to chip at the shiny spot on the wall.

If there was anything good there, we'll never know, because just at that moment there was a kind of rumbling sound. I think somebody yelled, "Run," but I had no chance to move. There was a sudden downpour of earth and rocks and rotted wood timbers. All I could do was cover my head as everything went black.

When I came to, I was lying face down on the floor of the mine shaft. It was hard and cold, and I was scared. I could see absolutely nothing. For some reason, it flashed into my head that it would be just like this in a grave—black and still—nothing.

It occurred to me there was a good chance this would *be* my grave.

My senses slowly cleared and I became aware of the dust in my mouth and nostrils. I'd have given anything for a drink of water. But my thirst quickly lost ground in importance to the pain I was starting to feel in the back of my head.

I tried to raise my right arm to feel my head, and got a shock. Something was holding my arm down! I made my befuddled brain work on the problem, I finally realized the falling dirt had landed on top of me. There was a long moment when I gave way to sheer panic. I was buried under the cave-in!

For the first time in my life, I experienced the kind of fear that can totally paralyze and control. I was shivering, and yet sweat was dripping down my face.

In my mind, I could see Mom and Dad and the rest of my family and friends. Would I ever get back to them?

With a start, I remembered I hadn't been alone in the cave-in. Luke, Brandon, and Matt were together somewhere near me, even further in. No doubt they were buried, too. Or worse. Maybe they were already dead. For all I knew, I was dying myself right now.

And Charlie. He'd been behind me, not quite as far along. Had he been close enough to the entrance to get out? Or had he been coming up behind me?

If all of us had been trapped inside the cave, it would be late tonight before anyone missed us and likely morning before they figured out what had happened and started digging. Chances were pretty grim that any of us would be alive.

My panic was replaced by a sick feeling in the pit of my stomach, and then gradually pain took over my thoughts. I'd been aware that my head was aching, but now I realized it was throbbing. And it wasn't only my head, but also my left arm and leg. I seemed to be surrounded by pain.

I decided I needed to find out how badly buried I was.

My face was against what I assumed was cold, hard dirt. I raised my head a bit. There was a stab of pain, but at least I could lift it. Next, I tried to lift my left arm. Pain shot through me and I quickly stopped any attempt to move it.

I'd already tried and failed to lift my right arm, but now I tried to drag it toward me. It didn't hurt, but it felt pinned down, and I couldn't pull it free.

Panicked at the thought of being unable to move at all, I used all my strength to push up. There was a tiny burst of dirt and rocks and suddenly, my right arm was free. But the dust made me sneeze, and that hurt. I also noticed that the air wasn't very good—musty and kind of stale. I wondered what it was like to be unable to breathe. I guess there'd be less painful ways to go.

I wondered again about the other guys. So far, the only noise I'd heard was what I'd made myself. I tried to call, but my voice sounded hoarse and all I got back was a bit of an echo.

I decided to see what my legs were like. I could tell that they were covered by something—dirt and rocks, I guessed—but I didn't yet know if I could pull myself out. So I felt around as well as I could with my right arm. My head and shoulders seemed to be free, but it felt as if there was a mountain of dirt and rocks on top of my back and my legs.

I realized that my phone was in my back pocket, but there was no way on earth I could reach it. Not that it would probably work anyway. Reception around here was hit or miss at the best of times.

I tried to pull myself forward. If I could get my back free, maybe I could somehow reach the phone… But the pain from my head and left arm forced me to stop, and, anyway, I knew I wasn't getting anywhere.

I felt the back of my head with my right hand. It was sticky—likely blood. I kind of raised myself up so I could try to feel my left arm. To my surprise, I discovered that it was only buried under a few inches of dirt. However, it hurt just to touch, so I gave up. It occurred to me that I might have landed on it when I fell, and maybe broken it. The less I moved, the less I hurt, so I cushioned my face against my right forearm and lay still.

Thoughts began to tumble through my head. I could see the headlines in the paper. "Teenagers Killed Because of Stupidity."

My family. What would they think? They trusted me not to do dumb things like this. All of us knew better. Why hadn't we used our brains?

Then I wished that I'd die. If the other guys were dead, I sure didn't want to be the only one to come out alive. How could I ever face their moms and dads? How could I explain what we were doing in the mine shaft? Better to be dead than have the whole town staring at me and talking about how stupid I was.

I started blaming Luke. After all, he was the one who'd been showing off for Charlie.

On the other hand, if it hadn't been for Charlie, Luke wouldn't have needed to show off. It was my fault Charlie had come. I'd known Luke wouldn't like it. Brandon and Matt were okay, but there was no reason to bring Charlie. This had been Luke's and my spot for several years. Before that, we'd camped by a stream near Luke's house. We'd been best friends forever—since even before grade one. We'd just kind of clicked.

Really, when you got right down to it, this was all Jamie's fault. If she hadn't been monopolizing Luke, I'd never have started spending my time with Charlie, and maybe none of this would have happened.

But then, I liked Charlie, too. I got a big kick out of watching him. He was a good friend. Better than Luke had been for the last few months.

I lay in the pitch-black mine shaft and started remembering that first day I'd met Charlie and how it had all started. It had all started because Mom asked me to take over the stupid cake....

Oh, what did it matter now anyway? We were trapped in a lonely, deserted mine shaft, and we'd likely never get out alive, so who cared how it had happened, or why? It had.

I had no way of knowing how long I lay there, now conscious only of the pain, then sleeping a while, then thinking about my family and the people I knew, wondering what they would say about me after they knew what had happened.... I heard something. It seemed to be coming from far away, but it was definitely some kind of noise. It got closer, and I realized there were several voices. They were muffled, and I wondered if they were coming from outside the mine. I hoped it was a rescue party and not just some kids. I tried to yell, but not much sound came out.

But the noise and the voices grew louder. They were coming into the mine!

In a few moments, I could see the flicker of lights, and then the shadows of people coming near.

I heard Charlie's voice. "Here he is! I couldn't tell how badly he was hurt because I had no light. Do you see any sign of the others?"

As Charlie knelt beside me, I saw lights playing on the mound of rubble that had buried all but my head and shoulders. The mine shaft was completely blocked! Where were Luke, Matt, and Brandon?

Charlie must have realized that my eyes were open. He said, "Are you okay? Sorry to leave you alone, but with no light, I couldn't do a thing."

"You're okay?" I asked weakly.

"Yeah, it missed me. When I realized I couldn't do anything here, I tried to call for help, but I couldn't get any reception. So I went back to the camp. It took me a little time to hot-wire the car, but I managed. I didn't know where to go for help. I didn't realize there were so few farms in this area. Anyway, we'll soon get you out."

He was digging away at the dirt while he talked, but new stuff kept sliding down. A man came over with a board, and they sort of used it like a dam to hold back the stuff on top. It wasn't long before they were able to ease me out.

Meanwhile, the other men were clearing away rubble from near the side where I'd last seen Luke and the others. It was slow, hard work.

With help from the others, Charlie and a man who said his name was Pete placed me on the board. They were careful not to jar my left arm, but it still hurt a lot. Then they carried me out of the shaft. Once outside, Pete gave me some tea from a thermos. Boy, did it taste good!

Charlie said these men were from farms in the area, but there was an ambulance on the way. He'd phoned my parents and asked them to call the others, so likely they'd all be here before long. Then Charlie went back into the mine.

Pete had been examining me while I drank the tea, and now he said he thought I'd be okay. He wound a bandage around my head. He said I'd been gashed by a falling two by four that had been used to shore up the mine to keep rocks from falling, and I'd likely need stitches. He put a splint on my left arm because he thought it could be broken. He did the same for my leg, but said he thought it was just bruised and maybe strained or something. When he was done, he left me there all wrapped up in blankets, and went back to help dig.

I realized I hadn't been in the mine nearly as long as I'd thought. From where the sun was, I figured it was about one o'clock. I'd been laying there maybe an hour at most.

Pete came out once to make sure I was okay, and then he went back in. They were having trouble because they didn't have a lot of equipment.

About ten minutes after I'd been brought out, I heard the sound of an ambulance siren, and soon I could see a trail of dust. Several cars were coming.

I saw the cars stop at the foot of the hill, and people get out. There were stretchers and shovels and bags of other stuff. People began moving up the side of the hill. It was a good fifteen-minute climb, but soon there were people everywhere. My dad was there. Mom had waited down at the car. Luke's and Brandon's dads had come. Matt's dad was away, but his brother-in-law was here.

Soon everyone was inside except my dad and the two ambulance men. The men checked me over and admired Pete's work, and then moved me to a stretcher so they could carry me down.

Dad alternated between yelling at me for going into the cave, being glad I was out, and worrying about the other guys. I was pretty worried myself.

The trip down the hill took forever. The paramedics didn't want to give me anything until I'd had my head x-rayed, so I had to grit my teeth and pretend I didn't notice the pain. Acting has never been one of my talents.

All the mothers waiting at the cars rushed over when they saw me, but, thankfully, Dad said I was in no shape to talk, so the guys just put me in the ambulance. Mom got in, too, and we were off. Dad said he'd stay and help dig.

Mom just held my good hand and didn't say anything. I knew she was crying, and to tell the truth, so was I. Luke and Matt and Brandon still hadn't been found.

About five minutes after we drove away, we passed another ambulance, its siren going strong.

It was a long drive back to town. I dozed off a few times, but each time I woke up, there was Mom, still holding my hand. It sure felt good.

When we got to town, I was wheeled into an x-ray room where they took pictures of my head, arm, and leg. After a while, I was bandaged and taped up like a mummy and sent to another room. Besides the ten stitches in my head, I had a slight concussion; my arm was fractured just below the elbow; and, as Pete had said, my leg had been twisted and bruised, but not broken. I had to stay in the hospital at least overnight to make sure my head was okay.

A few minutes after the nurse left me, Mom came in. She said, "Both ambulances got here just a few minutes ago."

Chapter 7

I hardly dared to breathe. "Are they——?"

"They're okay. Banged up, but they'll be back to normal soon."

I felt a great weight lift from my chest. "Oh, Mom, I was so scared."

"We all were." She came closer and hugged me as well as she could. "Your dad will be here in a few minutes. He helped Charlie clean up your camp, and then he went to get something for Mrs. Lovansky. She's been close to hysterics since we heard."

I understood that. Brandon's sister was killed in a freak car accident last winter. His mom would go crazy if anything happened to Brandon.

I guess I must have relaxed after that. When I woke up, it was dark outside. I was in a ward with other people, but the curtains around my bed were closed so I couldn't see anything. I tried to move, but gave up. It hurt too much.

As if she'd known I was awake, a nurse appeared and checked me and asked if I'd like a drink. I said, "Yes," and in a minute Dad was there holding a glass with a straw that bent over to let me drink without moving.

After I finished, he sat down and told me how they'd found the others about half an hour after I'd left in the ambulance. Luke had been next to the side wall and hadn't been hit by anything except dirt and small pebbles, so although he was trapped there, he was fine. He had some cuts and bruises, but he was okay. Brandon had a couple of cracked ribs. Matt had been hit by either some timber or a rock, and, like me, he had a concussion and a broken bone—in his case, his foot.

Then Dad said we were pretty lucky. The cave-in had been in a fairly small area. If it had been even a little bit wider, we'd all have been completely buried. Instead, one side of it had caught me and the other side caught them. Matt's head had actually been buried, and he'd been unconscious for a few minutes, but Brandon was close enough to claw the dirt away and help him get his face clear. So it looked like Brandon was the real hero.

After that, like me, all of them had been able to breathe. However, because we were trapped inside the cave with no fresh air coming in, we would have eventually used up the oxygen and it could have been much worse than it was.

Then Dad said, "Why on earth did you go in there? Charlie seems to be the only one of you with any sense. He says he realized at once that it was dangerous, so he stayed near the entrance. The next thing he knew he heard a yell and the sound of falling rocks. Why did the rest of you have to be so stupid? I thought I could trust you not to do anything as insane as that! You've all had your mothers nearly frantic with worry!"

What could I say? He was right. And I knew he was mostly mad because of how worried he'd been himself. So I didn't argue.

Dad ended with, "I sure hope you boys learned a lesson today. You're just lucky none of you got killed learning it."

I nodded.

I guess I must have looked the way I felt, because Dad suddenly laughed. "Okay, Glen, the storm's over. But please think before you do something foolish again."

I said I would.

Dad asked if I needed anything. When I said I'd probably go back to sleep, he agreed that was a good idea. He and Mom would come back in the morning and see if I could go home.

Then he was gone.

It was a while before I went to sleep. Living dangerously isn't something I normally do. I guess the truth is that I'm too lazy. Usually, getting into trouble takes more effort than I care to put out. This seemed like a late date to start doing stupid things. But then, I'd done several new things since Charlie arrived.

Speaking of Charlie, the next day I learned that he'd become an overnight hero.

As if he hadn't had enough attention before, now adults as well as girls and football fans thought he was the greatest thing to hit our town since television. Everybody knew who he was and how he'd saved the lives of four crazy teenagers. And wasn't it too bad there weren't more kids with sense?

Matt was stuck at home for a while because of the concussion and broken ankle, but by the next Saturday, we were all able to get around. However, we tried to be seen as little as possible. While everyone was glad we hadn't been badly hurt, they still found it necessary to make little digs about how dumb we'd been and how lucky we were and so forth. For that reason, I was glad the football game that week was out of town.

Luke and Charlie both played and they won again. Charlie was the hero yet again.

Luke was mad, according to him because a couple of times Charlie had kept the ball himself when Luke was in the open and Luke thought Charlie should have thrown to him. So Luke's ever-present dislike of Charlie gave way to a more intense hatred, made all the more unbearable because Luke realized that Charlie really might have saved his life.

I took pains to keep Charlie out of Luke's way.

Jamie helped. Coming home from the weekend away with her family, she was met with the news that Luke had almost got himself killed. She apparently took a vow never again to let him out of her sight. Luke was torn between wanting to have some space now and then, and gratification at having all her attention.

And Charlie? He just went on being his usual self. All he ever said to me was, "You shouldn't have gone in so far. I'm just glad I didn't."

When other people congratulated him, he shrugged them off, saying, "I only did what anyone would have done under the circumstances."

One thing I'd wondered about was the case of empty beer cans. I expected my dad to yell at me about that.

When I asked Charlie, he said, "Oh that. I took care of it when I went back to the camp. I just threw them in Luke's car and dumped them along the way when I went to find help. I thought they would just complicate things." Always thinking, that Charlie.

Auditions for the play were held on Tuesday, and as I expected, Charlie got the part of Algernon. Miss Carter actually gave Luke the opportunity to have the other male lead role even though he hadn't tried for it, but he turned it down. So she gave it to Greg Johnson, who isn't a great actor, but who at least would have the lines perfect. Marta and Paige Newbury got the main female parts and Nicole was Lady Bracknell. Zoey was Miss Prism, and Cal Ng the preacher.

The property and set crew had another meeting to figure out what we had to do and assign jobs. It was going to be a fair bit of work. Luke joined the sound crew, but he had no interest in it at all.

What effect the cave-in had on Nicole, I couldn't tell. The day I went back to school, she asked me how I was feeling, and I imagine she asked the others as well. She said she was glad we were all okay. But if she thought more of Charlie because of what he'd done, I saw no sign. Most girls chattered like magpies about it every time Charlie came near, but not Nicole. Not that I've ever seen her chatter like a magpie. She doesn't normally talk much. At least not at school. Or even at the youth group.

Speaking of that, I managed to avoid going to church the following Sunday. I pled hurting all over, which wasn't far from the truth, and spent the morning in bed.

My parents had had a week to wear out their emotions, so things were getting pretty well back to normal.

Fortunately, it was my left arm I'd broken, so I wasn't hampered too much. Unfortunately, I could still write, so my teachers assumed I was as capable (and as lazy) as ever.

There was a football game the next Saturday afternoon and there was a Halloween dance Saturday night. I told Charlie I'd go to it only if I could just watch. He laughed and said sure.

Then he reminded me about the youth group's Halloween party Friday night. He was helping get the old house decorated to be scary. I said I'd had enough dark scary places to last me a lifetime, but he laughed and somehow got me to say I'd go.

Since Nicole had told him she was going to the party with someone else, Charlie decided to go stag. He had some idea of not dating anyone else so she'd see how serious he was about her. I didn't mind, since I had no intention of asking a girl.

Anyway, Friday night we loaded up the car with hot dogs, buns, marshmallows and pop, and headed for the farm. It was about fifteen minutes east of town, and we left at six-thirty so we'd be early. I sat in the car listening to music while Charlie and two others guys—Ted and Kenny—finished decorating the house.

Then more cars started to arrive. Soon the farmyard was full of kids, and, of course, Mr. Reiss.

Most of the kids seemed to have come in couples, but not all of them. As far as I could tell, Nicole was with Derek Palmer. He's in grade 12, but in a different class. I neither know him very well or care to. He's the kind of person who's always sure he has the right answer even though half the time he's wrong.

The people in charge waited until everyone had arrived, and then Charlie opened the door. "Enter into the House of Horrors, folks. Step right in. Don't push. Don't be scared, ladies. We'll protect you."

Several girls giggled and said they weren't going inside. Nicole said, "Come on. It can't be that bad," and walked through the door. Derek followed her. In ones and twos the others went in. I was last. Charlie shut the door.

Inside, all was dark except for tiny luminous arrows pointing the trail. Up ahead, there were squeals and shrieks (mostly female) along with laughing (mostly male). To tell the truth, I thought it was all kind of silly. But that's me.

I followed along and got the usual treatment—something cold and clammy grabbing my head (it was a rubber sheet), some kind of gooey junk on the floor to make your feet stick (it took Mom half an hour to get it all off my shoes), an assortment of things dangling on strings, mirrors placed so you scared yourself, and ugly rubber creatures jumping out. I suppose as far as haunted houses go it would get a pretty high score. At least the kids, especially the younger ones, seemed to think so.

We finally arrived outside again. Charlie and Andy Parker had the campfire going and there were logs for sitting on and sticks for everyone. We sang songs for a while and then roasted wieners.

I noticed that Charlie was sitting on one side of Nicole and Derek on the other. They were both trying to get food and drinks for her and to occupy her attention. As far as I could tell, she was giving them equal time. She was smiling, as usual, but tonight it seemed to be forced—like she was trying to look happy, but if she'd been alone she'd have been sad. I figured maybe she wasn't feeling well.

I didn't try to sing, but I liked listening to the songs. Despite the hamper of the cast, I cooked a couple of hot dogs. That done, I sat on a log and drank a Coke.

After we'd eaten, Mr. Reiss talked for a while about disguises, and how most people use some kind of a disguise so other people won't know what they're really like inside. He talked about some people in the Bible who seemed to be really great, but who were rotten inside. I think he called them "hypocrites."

After he was finished, we roasted marshmallows over the coals. I ate a few and then I kind of wandered off.

It was a beautiful night—likely one of the last warm evenings we'd have. The fields around the farm were all taken care of, and the rows of turned topsoil looked like giant sleeping caterpillars. I walked toward a small stand of trees. There were a few birds singing and crickets chirping. Soon snow would cover the ground and the area would be virtually empty except for a few birds—not song birds—who would somehow manage to find food.

I sat down for a few minutes just to rest, but before long I realized a couple of cars were leaving. I got up and walked back. I had no desire to spend the night here—not without a sleeping bag.

By the time I got back, only three cars were left. Something seemed to be wrong with Derek's car, because he and Charlie and Mr. Reiss were all looking at the engine. Nicole was sitting alone on a log. I knew I wouldn't be much help with the car, so I decided I ought to be polite and at least attempt to talk to Nicole.

I sat down on a log near hers. "What's wrong?" I asked.

Nicole shrugged. "Something about the starter."

"Oh."

There was a pause. I said, "You don't look so good." I realized that sounded bad and tried to explain. "I mean—well, I don't mean you look bad or anything. You always look good. I just mean you look kind of sick." I was really making a mess of this. "I mean as though maybe you don't feel well."

She smiled a little. "Do I look terrible?"

"No, of course not. You look fine. Only maybe tired."

"I am a little tired."

There was a long pause. She said, "Did you enjoy all the stuff in the house?"

I felt embarrassed. "No."

"Neither did I."

"They did a lot of work on it."

"Most of the kids liked it."

"Yeah."

I looked over at Derek's car. The three were still bent around the engine. I walked over to them. From the conversation I overheard, I thought maybe they were enjoying themselves.

I got up my courage and spoke to Charlie. "Can I borrow your car? You could get a ride with Derek or Mr. Reiss."

Charlie looked surprised, but nodded, gave me the keys, and stuck his head back under the hood.

I told Derek I was taking Nicole home because she was tired. Derek glanced toward her, looked as though he was going to argue, looked at the engine, and said okay.

I returned to Nicole and told her I was driving her home. After a minute, she followed me to Charlie's car.

By now, I was feeling somewhat surprised at myself, but it made sense for me to take her home since neither of us wanted to sit around waiting.

We didn't talk much. I figured she had a headache. Mom gets them sometimes, and when she does all she wants is to be left alone.

I dropped her off at her house. She thanked me for bringing her home and I said it was no trouble and she went in.

Then I drove home, parked the car in Charlie's driveway, and went to bed.

The next day, I puttered around the house. With my arm the way it was, there weren't many things I could do. Mom said I could read some of my school books, so I did that for a while.

After lunch, I decided to walk over to Luke's. We hadn't really had a chance to talk since the cave-in.

I was a bit surprised to find him alone at home. He and Jamie were going out that night, so she was off having her hair done or something. His dad was at work, and his mom and sister were shopping. We ate some chips and drank Cokes, and then he started to let off some steam.

"Can you beat that guy?" He meant Charlie, of course. "It's like he's some kind of superman or something. It's weird. I mean, nobody's *that* perfect."

"You let him get to you."

"He sure does get to me."

"You're jealous."

I knew right away I shouldn't have said it, but the words sort of popped out.

Luke glared at me. "Of that—that—!"

"Forget it." I got up. "I didn't mean it."

"Oh, yes, you did. You think I'm jealous of that blond vacuum! You think he's better than me, don't you? You used to be my best friend, Glen Sauten, but now you're just one of Charlie's groupies—yeah, and likely the worst one. Well, don't waste your time coming to see me. Or did you just come to find out stuff so you and Charlie could have a big laugh?"

He was standing now, and getting madder by the minute. "Get out of here before I throw you out! I'd like to break your other arm for you!"

I left without bothering to point out that very little of what he'd said made any sense. I know Luke pretty well. He flies off the handle really fast, but I knew he'd soon calm down, and (I hoped) see how silly he'd been.

I realized I'd managed to get myself sort of caught in the middle. I didn't particularly want to stop being friends with Charlie, but Luke was going to be mad unless I did. On the other hand, Luke was so busy with Jamie he didn't have time to be much of a friend anyway, so there wasn't a lot of choice involved.

The football game was at four o'clock. Matt went with me, and we sat with some other guys from our class. Nicole was with Zoey and Andy Parker and Ted Bradden. They looked as though they were enjoying themselves. I guess she was over her headache.

We won again. To be perfectly honest, the team looked great.

As usual, Charlie was the star. Most of the cheering was for him.

After the game, I went home and ate and relaxed until Charlie picked me up for the dance. He was in great spirits until I mentioned seeing Nicole with Andy.

"What's with that girl, anyway? She's going to go someplace with me this week or I'm going to—I don't know what—kidnap her!"

I knew Charlie was joking. But I also knew he was really puzzled. He'd asked Nicole out a number of times now, and she'd never even hesitated before saying no. Didn't she like him? And if she didn't, why on earth not?

We went to the dance and Charlie seemed to have a good time dancing with one girl after another. A lot of them were pretty obviously crazy about him, and their admiration seemed to take any other thoughts from his mind. But not from mine. I leaned against the wall and kind of stared out at the dancers. The only two people in town (as far as I knew) who didn't like Charlie were Luke and Nicole.

Luke I could understand. For as long as I could remember, he'd been what you might call the most popular guy in our class. This year it was Charlie. Luke had counted on being quarterback. Instead, Charlie was doing the job and doing it well. And Charlie had won the part in the play that Luke wanted. So Luke had reasons to be jealous.

But what about Nicole? Was she interested in somebody else? Derek or Andy or one of the other guys? Even though none of them came close to Charlie.

But then there's no accounting for people's taste. I remember my sister was crazy about this loser Eddie

Denton before she met Ron. So maybe Nicole did like somebody else.

A movement on the floor attracted my attention. It was Luke. He was walking away from the dancers, and even from a distance I could see that he was mad. I looked past him and quickly figured out why. Jamie was dancing with Charlie. He must have cut in and she'd let him. I groaned. Didn't Charlie know how Luke felt about him?

I followed Luke outside.

He'd stopped on the steps and was taking some deep breaths.

I came up behind him. I wasn't sure what to say, especially after this afternoon.

"I'm glad you didn't hit him," I said at last.

"How could I? The slob saved my life two weeks ago."

"Makes it difficult, all right."

He half yelled, half laughed. "Oh, Glen, you're such an idiot."

"My dad says that, too, sometimes."

"I'm going out back. Coming?"

"What for?"

"Rick said he's got something in his car. I could use a drink."

Reluctantly, I followed him. I was glad Luke had gotten over being mad at me, but I didn't want him to start drinking. The last time he'd had a few, he'd wound up hitting Charlie and getting decked. I didn't want that to happen again.

I also knew what our parents would say if we got caught drinking when we were underage. After the cave-in, they'd hit the ceiling.

I had a couple of drinks from Rick's bottle and then said I had to go to the washroom. As soon as I got inside the building, I looked around for Jamie.

She was walking on the edge of the dance floor.

"He's out back," I said.

"What's he doing?"

"Drinking."

"The idiot! Is he mad?"

"What do you think?"

Jamie had to know how Luke felt about Charlie. The question was, how did Jamie feel about either of them? She demands almost slave-like devotion from the guy she goes with, but I don't know if she gives it in return.

"I'll go get him."

She left, and I breathed a sigh of relief. If anyone could talk Luke into a good mood, it was Jamie.

I settled back to resume watching the dance, but now everything seemed to get my goat. The music was too loud and you couldn't make out the words, and even when you could, hardly any of them made sense. I remembered the singing last night at the youth party. Now, that was more like songs ought to be. Like they meant something.

The air was getting to me, too. It was hot and sweaty, and there was too much laughter. It was all just a little bit forced. I remembered that bit about wearing a disguise, and I found myself wondering how many of the people here were wearing disguises. Not phony costumes, but faces or manners and stuff.

I wondered about me. Was I really what people saw or was there a different Glen Sauten hidden inside? It was a weird thought.

A hand touched my shoulder and I turned to find Charlie beside me. "You look as if you're in a different world, old man. Arm hurting?"

"No. Just—thinking."

"I saw you talking to Jamie. Luke mad at me?"

I nodded.

Charlie grinned. "I know I shouldn't have done it, but I couldn't resist. What's he always so mad about, anyhow?"

I shrugged. I didn't feel like discussing Luke with Charlie any more than I wanted to discuss Charlie with Luke.

"Sure a crowd here tonight. Have you changed your mind about finding a girl?"

"Nope."

"Want to go to the Diner?"

"Sure."

"Okay. Peggy's coming with us if you don't mind."

"Just as long as she's with you."

Charlie laughed. "You're going to grow up one of these days, and will you ever kick yourself over what you've missed."

I let that remark pass.

Peggy met us at the door with her coat. Charlie helped her put it on and then the three of us walked to the car. I offered to drive and Charlie looked at my arm. "Can you manage? But, then, you did pretty well last night, didn't you?"

So I drove while Peggy told Charlie how great he is.

The Peabody Diner was fairly crowded. I went inside and stood in line to get our order. When it was ready,

Charlie came and carried it to the car. We had the CD player on with a new saxophone disc I liked. Unless Charlie spoke to me, I kind of drifted with the music.

Afterwards I drove around for a while. To tell the truth, I was feeling kind of in a bad humor. I guess I'm sort of the opposite of Luke. I hardly ever get angry. It just doesn't seem to be in me. But now and then I kind of slowly build up until I get good and mad. It doesn't happen much. Hardly ever.

I do remember once getting mad at a couple of kids who were tormenting a cat. I just lit into them. They creamed me, but at least the cat got away.

Anyway, for some reason I kind of felt like I was on the edge of getting mad now, but I really didn't know why. All I knew was that Charlie and Peggy were getting on my nerves.

I realized I'd driven to our street. I pulled into my drive and put the car into park. "Sorry, folks. Your chauffeur just retired for the night."

Chapter 8

Charlie got out of the back seat, and Peggy moved over and smoothed her hair.

Charlie said, "Okay, Glen. I thought you were feeling tired. You get yourself a good night's rest and I'll see you in the morning."

I said, "Yeah, sure," and headed for the house.

The key was in the mail box as usual. I knew Mom would be listening for me to come in. I stopped and watched as Charlie helped Peggy into the front seat and drove away. I looked over at his house. It was pitch black. His folks were likely out.

I stumbled in and got a glass of milk from the fridge. After I drank it, I brushed my teeth and started struggling to get my clothes off. It's hard to do with one hand, especially when you're tired. But then Dad was there, helping me get undressed, finding my pajamas, and turning off the light. I fell asleep at once.

I was still in bed when Charlie arrived the next morning. Mom came in to wake me up and ask if I wanted to stay in bed or go to church. I knew she was still puzzled about the whole church bit, but she hadn't asked outright. Maybe she figured you shouldn't complain if your kid starts going to church.

Given the choice—and not having to face Charlie—I was surprised to discover that for some strange reason I actually felt like going. I'd been away two weeks, and I almost felt as if I'd missed something.

I got my clothes more or less on—putting on socks with one hand is a bit of a challenge—and Mom tied my shoes while I grabbed some toast. Mom and Dad talked to Charlie. It turned out his parents were away for the weekend at some medical conference. Mom asked why on earth he hadn't said so and come over to our house. She told him he was certainly welcome to come back for lunch, and he said he'd like to do that.

We found a place to sit about halfway down, fairly close to where Nicole's family generally sits. Sure enough, they came in and sat in front of us. Charlie gave them all his biggest smile. Mrs. Grant smiled back.

I didn't hear much of the sermon. I was still feeling tired after the night before. I guess I didn't listen in the youth group either. I'm not sure where my mind was; I only know where it wasn't.

When it was over, I went outside to wait for Charlie.

He was a while coming. After the successful Halloween party, not to mention the football game, the kids all wanted to talk to him.

"You okay?" Charlie asked when he finally came out to the car.

"Yeah," I said. "Just tired, I guess."

"Not that you usually break records for hysterical behavior, but you seem to be someplace else lately. What's the matter? Did your life flash before your eyes in that mine, and you've finally realized how dull it is?"

I grinned. "No. Just being around you is as much excitement as this small-town boy can handle."

He laughed. "I have to admit living in a small town isn't quite as bad as I'd expected. Of course," he added, "my expectations weren't all that high."

We went to our house for lunch. Mom had made a bacon quiche and a Caesar salad, along with a good old-fashioned apple crisp. Charlie asked if she'd like to cater to his house whenever his folks were away.

Mom laughed.

He said he wasn't joking, and she could name her own price.

She said when his folks were away, he should just come over and stay with us.

Then we cleaned up and did the dishes. I should say *they* did. One good thing about my arm's being out of commission was that I got out of a lot of chores. Of course, I knew Mom would probably just save a lot of them for later. But, still, it was one plus.

Charlie and Dad had a couple of games of Ping-Pong. They split. Then Charlie asked me to go to the diner with him. It turned out he wanted to talk. "So, Glen. What do you think?"

"About what?"

"Nicole, of course. That girl is beginning to get to me. Did you see her on Friday night? It's the same at our play rehearsals. No matter what I say to her, she never argues or anything. Half the time I'm not even sure she hears me. And Derek! What on earth does she see in him? He's a creep!"

"Yeah."

"Don't you think so?"

"Well, I've never had much to do with him. He acts like he's better than anybody else, but he's really a loser."

"So why does Nicole want to be around him? How long has she been dating him, anyway?"

"Off and on for a couple of years. Not a lot. At least, not that I know. I don't think she goes out much with anybody."

"But she's been asked, right?"

"Sure. Most of the guys have asked her out. Luke did a couple of times."

"But it was no go, huh?"

"Nope. She just goes out sometimes with Derek or Ted or Andy."

"Well, Ted or Andy I can stand. I mean, they're as dull as pieces of cauliflower, but they aren't creeps. Not that I can see why she'd go out with them, either."

"I dunno."

Charlie leaned toward me. "Glen, we've got to figure this out." He spoke so earnestly I knew it was really a big thing to him. "I'm going to get Nicole Grant to go out with me if it's the last thing I do!"

I shifted somewhat uncomfortably in my seat. "Well, there are a lot of other girls. Likely any of them would date you."

He shrugged. "So what? Where's the challenge? None of them can hold a candle to Nicole, and you know it."

"Yeah, I guess."

"What we need is a new strategy. I've tried a couple of things, but they haven't worked. I can't figure out why. But we have to think of something else."

I was definitely uncomfortable now. "Charlie, I don't think I can help you. I mean, I know next to nothing about girls."

He waved that aside. "You've known Nicole longer than I have. You might remember something that would help." He drank some of his Coke and sat there deep in thought. Finally he turned toward me again. "I figured going to church and the youth group and all that would do it. I can't understand her at all. Her mother seems friendly and so does her dad. But she's barely polite. Polite! To me—Charlie Thornton!"

I didn't say anything. While I thought Charlie was kind of making a big deal of it, at the same time I could see his point of view. I mean, if I were a girl, I'd sure rather date him than Derek Palmer or Ted Bradden or pretty well any of the guys around here. He had brains, looks, money, and a sharp car, and he was what my mother would call sophisticated. At least, he was compared to the rest of us. So I was as puzzled as Charlie was over why Nicole wouldn't go out with him. But I could probably sit here for eighty years and still not have a single helpful idea about what he should do.

"There's got to be something I've missed!" Charlie hit the steering wheel with his fist.

"Maybe she only likes guys dumber than her."

"Women don't think that way. Just men."

"Oh."

"There has to be something!"

Just then, Marta drove her dad's car into the parking lot. She honked, then parked and came over. "Hi, Charlie Thornton. Or are you too busy to talk to me?"

"You know I'm never too busy to talk to you, Marta."

"I figured since you did your hero bit maybe your head had grown too big to let you talk to us ordinary mortals. But then I see you're here with Glen. Teaching him about how rocks fall?"

I sank lower in my car seat.

"Now, Marta. Don't rub it in," Charlie said, grinning. "You know, I'd much rather have rescued a beautiful damsel in distress—like you for instance."

"But I *am* in distress." She pouted. "I'm all alone and I'm bored. Any suggestions?"

Charlie winked at me. "Well, I could let Glen here drive my car, and then I could let *you* take me for a drive. That is, if you'd like to do that."

Of course, she agreed. Charlie made a big show of handing me the keys, and then he got out and walked with Marta to her car.

He had his arm around her waist and they were both laughing when the Grants' car drove into the parking lot and pulled up a couple of spots from Marta's. Nicole was driving, and there's no way she could have missed seeing them.

She had her younger sisters and another little girl with her, and they all got out and went inside.

I saw Charlie look back at her as if wondering what to do, but he must have decided to stay put because he kept laughing as he got into Marta's car and she drove off.

I sat in the Mustang finishing my milkshake. Nicole and the younger girls got ice cream cones and then started back to their car. The girls got in, but Nicole slowly walked over and spoke through my open window. "Hi, Glen."

"Uh, hi."

"Charlie deserted you?"

What could I say? "Uh, not exactly. Marta sort of needed some help, so he told me to drive his car home. I don't mind."

"Is your arm hurting?"

"Naw, it's okay."

"I thought maybe it hurt. At church this morning you seemed to be—well, not there, I guess."

I laughed, but I know my face was going red, as it always did. "Well, that's not unusual. I spend a lot of time like that at school."

She didn't laugh. "You really should try to concentrate, you know. That's one thing you could learn from Charlie that would help you."

Now what was that supposed to mean? And what was it to her, anyway? I didn't answer and she must have been embarrassed because she said, "I'm sorry. That's none of my business, is it? Well, I'd better be going."

She left me still trying to think of something to say. Why did I have to act like such an idiot around girls? If Charlie'd been here, he'd have found plenty to say to her! Maybe I should ask Charlie to do some tutoring. And not in how to get better marks at school, either!

Disgusted with myself, I drove home.

Charlie's parents were still away, so I kept the car keys.

Our house was empty, too, but the car was there. Mom and Dad had probably gone for a walk.

I wandered aimlessly through the rooms. For some reason I was mad. I put on the TV and tried to watch a golf tournament, but that only made me remember I couldn't play golf or anything else for a while. I switched it off.

What on earth was bugging me—first last night and then now? I couldn't remember having ever felt like this before.

At last, I pulled out a book we had to read for school. As usual, I'd been putting it off. I forced myself to follow the plot. Fortunately, it was a war story and almost interesting.

I was still reading when my parents got home. They were both pleased to see me with a book, but I told them reading was almost the only thing I could do and not to get their hopes up.

We were sitting down to dinner when Charlie came to get his keys. Mom found out his parents weren't back yet and insisted he eat with us. She didn't have to do much convincing.

After dinner, Dad helped Mom clean up and Charlie and I went downstairs.

He wanted to talk again. "Did you see Nicole today?"

"Yeah."

"Ten dollars says she saw me with Marta."

"She couldn't have missed you."

"So what do you think? Is she jealous?"

I blinked. "Jealous?"

"Sure. Don't you get it? The best way to get a girl interested in you is to make her think you aren't interested in her. Right?"

"You're asking me?"

"It has to work! She won't date me because she thinks she's already got me hooked, but as soon as she sees I know there are other fish in the sea, she'll start wondering what she's missing. I've got it all figured out!"

It sounded logical. But I thought of a flaw. "Wait a minute. You've been dating other girls all along and going to dances and all. Don't you think she knows that?"

He thought about it. "Maybe not. After all, she doesn't get around much. I doubt if she's even seen me with another girl. Other than talking to one at school, of course. Anyway, so what if she has? If I start acting like I'm really crazy about somebody else and I don't ask her out any more, she'll get the message, and she'll come after me. You just watch. Today with Marta was an accident, but just wait until I really get into action!"

I didn't say anything more. If life was so interesting now that Charlie was around, how come I had this weird feeling in the pit of my stomach?

Monday morning dawned crisp and clear. It was the kind of day that just begged for a shotgun and a retriever and a walk through the autumn woods to find grouse or pheasants. But all I could look forward to was another boring day in school. Not that I had a retriever; and I'd never shoot an animal or a bird, but there it was.

I forced myself to get up. Charlie knocked on the door before I was through breakfast. He was obviously all raring to go on his plan to make Nicole jealous.

As we drove into the parking lot, Charlie laughed quietly. "Maybe I could start there."

I looked around to see what he meant and saw Luke and Jamie. I glanced at Charlie and, sure enough, that's who he was looking at.

"Don't you dare!" I whispered.

He laughed as we walked toward them.

Luke promptly grabbed Jamie's arm and half-dragged her through the door. Yep, Luke was still mad.

I sighed.

We followed them inside and got our books organized. Sophie came by and stopped to talk to Charlie. I could almost hear his thoughts as he weighed the pros and cons of using Sophie to make Nicole jealous. Somehow, it didn't seem very fair to Sophie. But then I didn't owe her anything. She'd never done a thing for me over the years.

Anyway, Charlie must have made a decision, because he saw Marta out of the corner of his eye, said he'd talk to Sophie later, and ran to walk with Marta. Sophie stood there looking like she could kill somebody, and I quickly took myself out of her reach.

It made sense for it to be Marta. After all, he'd been with her yesterday when Nicole saw them. I had no difficulty with the choice. Marta had sneered at me so many times in the past it would be a pleasure for me to watch her get some of it back.

But I sure hoped Charlie knew what he was doing. If Marta ever found out she was being used to make Nicole jealous, there'd be awesome fireworks. I made a mental note to watch from a safe distance.

Right now, though, I hurried into class.

For some reason, Mr. Jackman was in a worse mood than usual. Maybe he wanted to get out into the woods, too. I could easily picture him shooting a grouse. Anyway, all

Charlie was doing was smiling, and he got told to wipe the grin off his face and get to work. I made it look as if I was busy. If he was going to yell at a top student like Charlie, there was no telling what he'd do to me.

He gave us some reading to do, and then he just sat at his desk. He seemed to be staring into space. It wasn't like him, but he wasn't the kind of person you questioned.

About halfway through the period, I took another quick look, and I saw that there were tears on his face. I just stared.

Someone moved, and I saw Nicole walk up to him and say something. He looked at her and then brushed his face with his handkerchief and stood. For a full minute, he stared around the room at us. At last, he spoke. "You're so young, all of you. So young." He walked out of the room.

Somebody made a dumb joke, but nobody laughed.

Nicole went back to her desk and sat down. I'd seen tears in her eyes. In fact, several of the girls were close to tears. It was so strange. You don't expect something like this in the middle of your history class.

I turned a bit and looked at Charlie. He raised his eyebrows. "What do you think that was all about?" I whispered.

"Search me. For once, I don't have an answer."

I smiled. True modesty.

For about five minutes, we all kind of talked quietly. One or two paper airplanes made a feeble effort to liven things up, and Doreen yelled, "Stop that!" when Bobby grabbed something from her desk. But most of us just kind of waited to see what would happen next.

Finally, the door opened and our principal, Mr. Kennard, came in. All eyes were on him as he stood at the front and cleared his throat. "Now, class, I expect you realize that Mr. Jackman is, er, not quite himself today. You're old enough to accept that. He's asked to take the day off. I understand it's a family matter and doesn't directly involve him. You realize that's all I can say. Since we have a few minutes left in this period, why don't you find some work to do? I'm sure you all have something."

We all made as if we were working for the rest of the class, but it was a relief when the bell finally rang and Mr. Kennard left. The second he'd gone through the door, the room was abuzz. Everybody had some wild idea about what was wrong, and everybody thought everybody else's ideas were crazy.

Charlie didn't waste time speculating. He made for Marta, and put his arm around her shoulder as they headed down the hall. As luck would have it, Nicole and Zoey were walking right behind them. But Nicole didn't appear to even notice. I guess she was worried about Mr. Jackman.

To tell the truth, I was a little worried myself. Not that I liked him or anything, but, well, you get used to people, and I was used to his being a tough nut. This morning, I guess you could say a crack had appeared. I didn't like that. Also, as I said before, his wife is a good friend of my mom's. If there was a family problem, it would involve her.

Because we had a math test the next day, Charlie thought we should go straight home. We went to his house and got Cokes. His mom had just arrived home from shopping, and she'd bought a frozen cake. My mom never buys them; she makes her own. Somehow, I couldn't quite see Charlie's mom with a messy kitchen or with flour in her hair or on her nose like my mom sometimes has. Still, the cake tasted pretty good. Well, sort of good.

When Charlie said he should start studying, I went home. I could have stayed, and he likely would have helped me, but I wasn't quite up to it. I'd had a hard day.

I'm not much for worrying. In fact, my family would say one of my problems is that I never worry about anything. But I was worried now.

First, I had Charlie walking on a tightrope trying to get Nicole to like him by pretending he'd fallen for Marta. Then I had Mr. Jackman and whatever was making him act like a human being. Finally, I had my former best friend beating his head against the brick wall who was my present best friend, and if I knew Luke, he wasn't about to lose gracefully.

And how I was supposed to calmly sit down—like Charlie—and study for a math test was more than I knew!

Mom was home. The first thing I did was ask her if she knew what was wrong at the Jackmans'. But she hadn't heard anything. She phoned another friend of hers, but no luck. She didn't know whether to phone Mrs. Jackman or not, so she decided to leave it for now.

"How's the play going?" she asked me as I grabbed a couple of scones out of the muffin tin.

"Okay, I think. We have our property list done and we're gathering stuff. I might need to take a few things from here."

"And the actors? Are they learning their parts."

"Yeah. They seem to be doing fine."

"You aren't sorry you didn't try out for a part?"

"No way. That's work!"

She put her hands on her hips. "Well, it would be nice if someday you'd stop being afraid of a little work!"

Chapter 9

I waited a minute to see if she was going to say anything more. Apparently not. She said she was going down to see our neighbour, Mrs. Pearson. I finished eating and tried to settle down to do some studying.

I wasn't worried about what Mom had said. I figured she was just worried about the Jackmans and had yelled at me because I was handy. No big deal.

Studying math was hard. Finally, I gave up and watched some TV.

Even after dinner I found it hard to concentrate. So when the phone rang I jumped for it. It was Charlie. He'd finished his homework and wanted to go down to the Diner.

I caught a look on Mom's face as I ran out the door. She was still exasperated with me.

We drove to the Diner and got hamburgers, fries, and root beer. We sat in the car.

"So, Glen, ready for the test?"

I groaned.

"Okay, we'll talk about something else." Then he got a puzzled expression on his face. "But seriously, why not do some studying? Good marks never hurt anyone, you know."

"You sound just like my mother," I complained.

He laughed. "Nobody's ever said I sounded like a mother before."

In an effort to change the topic, I said, "What do you think of the weather we've been having?"

He laughed again. "Wasn't that a riot with Mr. Jackman this morning? Man, I wanted to laugh. Did you see Nicole? She was crying! What a crazy female!"

I took a bite of my hamburger so I couldn't answer.

That night, I dreamed I was standing like a statue in the middle of a cave and rocks were falling on all sides of me. I could see the opening of the tunnel, but for some reason I couldn't move. It was as if I was glued there. Weird stuff! I woke up to pouring rain. A good day for a math test.

We had math first period, and the test was all I expected and then some. Maybe if I'd studied more, I wouldn't have felt so stupid when I looked at the test page and realized I didn't know how to do half the questions.

Afterwards, I asked Charlie what he'd thought of the test and he said he'd aced it. He likely had, too.

Charlie sat with Marta at lunch, so I joined Matt and Brandon.

Brandon said right off, "Luke's pretty mad, huh?"

"Yeah?" I tried to sound uninterested.

"Yeah. He's spreading rumors about Charlie. Says they moved here because he was expelled from his last school."

"Charlie expelled? That I'd like to see. What did they expel him for? Being too popular?" I shook my head. "Give me a break. Don't you guys know Luke is just jealous of Charlie?"

"That's what Luke said you'd say," replied Matt. "He says you're so glad Charlie lets you be his friend that you'd lick his boots for him."

"That jerk!"

"Charlie?" Brandon asked innocently.

"Tell Luke that I think Charlie is worth ten of him!"

"Tell him yourself," said a cold voice behind me.

I got out of the chair slowly and turned so I could face Luke. It didn't take a long look to know he was furious.

"Now, Luke—" was all I got out before he hit me. I wasn't expecting him to do anything quite that idiotic, so I took the full force of the punch and fell backward, clutching at the table with my good arm.

Brandon and Matt jumped up and grabbed Luke, or else he might have hit me again.

A bunch of other kids, Charlie and Marta included, rushed over to see what was going on, and so did Mr. Grange, who was the cafeteria supervisor.

"All right, what's this all about?" he demanded.

I looked over at Luke.

Charlie stood beside me, facing Luke.

"Uh, nothing," I said to Mr. Grange. It hurt to talk. "I was getting up and I fell over my chair."

Several people laughed and Marta made a comment about clumsy oafs, but nobody else spoke.

I was afraid Mr. Grange might pursue it, but maybe he didn't want to be bothered. He just said, "Be more careful in the future," before going back to his coffee.

Charlie stepped toward Luke. "I've got a funny feeling Glen was covering for you," he said. "From now on, if you want to start some trouble, you come to me."

He turned his back on Luke and took my arm. "Come on, we'll see if the phys ed department has an ice pack."

Luke brushed Brandon and Matt aside and stormed out through the far door.

I walked beside Charlie, with Marta tagging along.

"So, what was that all about?" Charlie asked when we were in the hall.

"Nothing, really." I shrugged. "He was in a bad mood and I was handy. That's all."

"I thought you and Luke were supposed to be best friends," Marta said. "What happened? Did he realize what a jerk you are?"

Charlie stopped dead.

Marta and I stopped, too.

"Look, Marta," Charlie said evenly, "Glen is a very good friend of mine and if you're going to make comments like that, you're going to find yourself looking for another date this Friday."

If she was surprised by Charlie's statement, she took it well. "Love me, love my pal, huh?"

"You've got it."

She started to laugh. "You guys take everything so seriously. You don't appreciate a little humor." She rolled her eyes. "Glen's such an easy guy to kid, and I've known him most of my life. He knows I don't mean anything."

"Yeah, it's okay," I mumbled through the pain in my jaw.

Charlie seemed satisfied. He took Marta's hand, and we went to the phys ed office where Mr. Wilton administered ice. It was obvious he didn't for one minute believe my story about falling into a table, but he just said, "Boys will be boys," and left it there.

When I went into physics class everybody stared at me, so I knew they'd all heard some version of what had happened. I glanced at Luke, but he started looking for something in his desk.

Somehow, I made it through that class and the study period afterwards. When the final bell rang, I left the room so quickly I almost bumped into Nicole outside the door. She hadn't looked well all day, and I thought maybe she was still worried about Mr. Jackman, who wasn't at school. Anyway, she seemed to be standing just outside the study room door and I barely kept from plowing right into her.

"Oh, Glen!" she said in surprise. "I—I was wondering how you were. They said you had a fight with Luke. I know that couldn't be true, could it?" She looked at me with those earnest green eyes, and I couldn't think of anything to say.

"Uh, well—uh—it was nothing. Not a fight. Really!"

"I'm glad to hear that. Was—was Charlie involved?"

So that's what this was about. She was worried about Charlie. It looked as if his strategy was working.

"No," I said. Then, for good measure, I added, "He and Marta were at a different table."

"Oh," was all she said. "Well, I'd better go."

She took off, and I went toward the side door where Charlie had parked. Charlie was driving Marta home, so I climbed in the back.

They wanted to go to Harry's Restaurant, but my jaw was aching so Charlie drove me home first.

"What are you going to tell your mother?" Charlie asked as I started to get out.

"I dunno."

"Think she'll swallow the table story?" Marta asked.

"No," I replied truthfully. "I'll tell her what really happened."

"That's a good idea," Charlie said. He was beginning to sound so fatherly I almost expected a "my boy" at the end.

"Yeah." I got out and went into the house.

For once, luck was on my side; nobody was home. Mom had left a note saying she was over at the Jackmans' and I should take the casserole out of the fridge and put it into the oven at four-thirty.

I set the buzzer to remind me of the time and stretched out on the couch in the living room. I relaxed on its cool firmness and was asleep in seconds.

The buzzer's drone woke me from a deep sleep and I stumbled to the kitchen, turned the oven to 350° and put the casserole in. That done, I went back to the couch and again drifted off to sleep.

I didn't wake up again until I heard our front door open.

Mom came into the room, and I could tell right away that she was upset.

"Glen, did you get my note?"

"Yeah, it's taken care of."

"Good." She sat down on the edge of a chair. "Well, I was over at the Jackmans'."

"You said that in your note."

"You know they have two sons?"

I sat up. "Yeah."

"The oldest, Frank, went to school with your sister, Jeanne, so he's about twenty-six."

"Yeah?"

"Glen, he's dying! They just talked to him Sunday night. He told them he has about six months to live. Maybe less. And there's nothing the doctors can do."

"Wow!"

"Now you know why Tom—Mr. Jackman—was so upset. He's just overwhelmed. Myra doesn't know what to do either. It's a terrible blow to both of them."

"Yeah."

"Anyway," Mom said as she got up and put her purse away, "we'll have to do what we can for them. But right now, I guess I'd better finish dinner."

"Yeah." I followed her to the kitchen and set the table without being asked.

No wonder he'd been so different. Sometimes it's hard to remember that teachers are people, too. I mean, they have lives and families that have no connection to the school. Only we don't often see them as human. Especially ones like Mr. Jackman. I didn't think I'd ever be able to think of him as I had before.

During dinner, Mom and Dad talked quite a bit about the Jackmans. I was pretty quiet.

It wasn't till the end of the meal that Dad noticed my face. "Glen, you've got a bruise there. In fact, it looks swollen. What did you do?"

I was ready for this. "Nothing, really," I said matter-of-factly. "Luke overheard me say something and he got mad and hit me."

"Luke?" Dad sounded surprised.

"At school?" Mom asked.

"Yeah."

"Where was the teacher?"

"It was at lunch time." I shrugged. "It's no big deal."

"Why would Luke hit you?" Dad asked.

"He said some dumb stuff about Charlie, and I told Brandon and Matt that Charlie's better than Luke, and Luke heard me."

"I don't see why the three of you can't all be friends," Mom said.

Dad said, "Why would you say that Charlie is better than Luke?""

"Because Charlie *is* better than him," I said. "He's better at playing baseball, basketball, and football. And he gets better marks. And Charlie beat Luke out for the lead part in the school play. And he's going to date a girl Luke couldn't. And Luke is jealous!"

"Oh," Mom said.

"I don't think that's necessarily all true," Dad said, "and even if it is, there must be other things Luke does better. But if the rivalry is between them, why do you seem to be caught in the middle?"

Good question. I wish I knew the answer.

"I guess because I like both of them." I sighed. "And I think they might even get along if Luke wouldn't act like such an idiot."

Mom was looking closely at my jaw. "Did you see the doctor?"

"Aw, Mom, it's nothing."

Dad took me over to the hospital and I sat in Emergency for quite a while before Dr. Thornton came and had a look at me. It was the first time I'd seen him at work, so to speak, and I decided he was probably very

good at what he did. He checked out my jaw and sent me
to have X-rays taken, but when he was sure it was only
bruised, he told me to work on my defense and sent me
home.

I had English and physics homework. It was hard to
concentrate, but I got it more or less done and was trying to brush my teeth before going to bed when Charlie
called.

"How's the jaw?" he asked.

"Fine."

"Good. Just thought I'd check. Guess who was at
Harry's after school?"

"Luke?"

"Nope. Miss Iceberg herself. She was with Zoey and
Darlene. I figured it was a good opportunity, so I made
like I was nuts over Marta."

"Oh?"

"I gave her lots to think about."

"Yeah."

"Anyway, see you in the morning."

"Yeah, and no jokes, okay?"

He laughed. "You'll get enough."

"By the way, Mom found out what's wrong with Jackmans."

"Yeah? What?"

"Their oldest son is dying. They just found out."

There was a brief pause. "I figured it was something
like that. Well, it happens all the time. Nothing to lose
any sleep over. See you tomorrow."

I didn't move for a few minutes. Maybe death didn't
mean a lot to a doctor's family. I mean, they must have

to get used to it. And Charlie'd only known Mr. Jackman for a short while. Still, I kind of wished I could talk to somebody who understood how I felt—kind of helpless.

I wondered if Luke would feel that way, or if he was too caught up in himself to feel anything right now.

I remembered the tears in Nicole's eyes on Monday. She might understand. Not that I'd ever say anything to her.

Charlie had thought her tears were silly. I didn't.

By Thursday, the whole school knew about Mr. Jackman's son's illness. Everyone talked about it during the breaks, but not openly.

Mr. Jackman was still absent.

I got through the rest of the week. Play practices were heating up and people were walking around with their scripts, trying to get their lines memorized. But I had nothing to worry about. Props isn't a high pressure area. Not that I was able to do much since my left arm was still in a cast.

Of course, Charlie couldn't concentrate wholly on the play because there were still a few more football games.

Things were looking good for our team. We were in first place and looked like a shoo-in for the championship for our area.

But in the game Saturday, Luke fumbled two passes he should have caught.

Charlie got mad and yelled at him. Luke shrugged.

In the fourth quarter, when we were behind by two points, Luke dropped a ball on the three-yard line.

Charlie was livid. He insisted that Luke dropped it on purpose. Whether he did or not I don't know, but the coach took Luke out of the game.

We won because Charlie got a touchdown himself. The other team made it all the way back to our five-yard line, but ran out of time.

I learned later that right after the game Charlie went into the locker room and apologized, in front of everyone, for accusing Luke of dropping the ball on purpose.

Luke, who had already showered and dressed turned way, picked up his duffel bag, and walked out.

I was standing just outside the locker room door when Luke came out.

"Get out of my way!" he snarled, grabbing my good arm and pushing me backward into the wall.

Jamie came up, still dressed in her cheerleader outfit. Her eyes flashing, she yelled, "Don't be an idiot, Luke!"

Right then Charlie and several others from the team came out of the locker room. Charlie grabbed Luke's shoulder and spun him around. Luke swung his heavy duffel bag, knocking Charlie backward into the other guys. Then he left, with Jamie running after. We could hear her yelling at him.

Now Luke had the whole team mad at him.

Truth to tell, there were a lot of spectators who thought it likely Luke *had* dropped at least one ball on purpose. His dislike of Charlie had really gotten out of hand for him to do a thing like that.

At the game the following week, there was no sign of Luke. Apparently he'd also missed two practices. Playing without him, they managed to win a squeaker, 15-14. Charlie was head and shoulders better than anyone else, but with Luke playing we likely would have had a more decisive (and less anxious) win.

Charlie continued to pay all kinds of attention to Marta, especially if Nicole was around. But we also went to church to keep Nicole's family happy.

What with football, rehearsals, work on the set, and schoolwork piling up, the weeks flew by.

Mr. Jackman was back and seemed almost grouchy enough to be his old self, except I was aware of an aura of sadness that hung around him. He would never really be his old self again.

I saw Nicole at Harry's once with Ted, but she looked tired. Like Mr. Jackman, she seemed somehow sad, though there was nothing tangible.

At church the week before the championship game, Mr. Reiss talked about being afraid to die. He read something about a man named Paul who said he didn't care whether he was dead or alive, because if he was dead he'd be with God, and if he was alive, he'd be pleasing God by doing his will.

It didn't make a lot of sense, but it got me wondering about Frank Jackman. Was he afraid to die? How would it feel to be told you only had a few months to live?

On the Wednesday night before the big game, I was watching TV and working on a few props for the play when Charlie came over. He sighed as he sank into a chair. "Luke wasn't out for practice again. The coach was going over to his house to talk to him."

"What a moron!"

"Not that we can't win without him—" Charlie got more animated "—but it would be nice to have somebody who can be relied on to catch balls and run well. Why can't he be content with being the second best player? Should I play badly just to make him feel good?"

"Of course not." There was a pause. I ended it with a chuckle. "Too bad it isn't as easy to make Nicole jealous as it is Luke."

Charlie laughed. "What makes you think it isn't? Have you seen her lately? She looks like she lost her best friend."

"Huh?" I looked at him. "I know she hasn't been like herself lately. But somehow I never even thought it was because of—well, you and Marta. But I guess that makes sense."

"Sure, it does. I figure I'll get her alone one of these days and tell her it's really her I'm crazy about, and she'll fall into my arms, and that'll be it."

"Well, maybe."

"Maybe, nothing. It's a sure thing."

There was silence for about a minute. I said, "Charlie?"

"Yes?"

"Do you ever think about dying?"

"Do I ever think about dying? What on earth is going on in your head? I thought you told me you never had serious thoughts?"

"Well, Mr. Reiss said something on Sunday about knowing whether you were afraid to die or not. I'd never thought much about it until the cave-in. Now, with Mr. Jackman's son—"

"Well, cut it out. There's plenty of time to think about things like that when the problem comes up. You don't need to waste valuable time now."

I didn't say any more. Maybe he was right. What good did it do to waste my time worrying about something that might not happen to me for sixty years? There was still a small nagging doubt, but I silenced it. We spent the rest of the time talking about football and the play.

There was a pep rally Friday at two-thirty. The whole team was there in uniform, except Luke. He was nowhere to be seen. Jamie was there, though, leading the cheer-leaders. The rumor was they'd had a fight over his not playing.

The football final the next day was a good one. As expected, we played the Riverside Rattlers, the team that had beaten us last year. This season, we'd beaten them 45 to 24 with Luke, and lost to them 32 to 27 without him. At half-time, the score was 14 to 7 for them. Their defense was holding tough, and Charlie had been sacked twice. He was doing his best, but what was needed was somebody who could catch the ball and do something with it—somebody like Luke.

But after the half, Charlie took matters into his own hands. He ran for a touchdown, but Joel missed the convert, so the score was 14 to 13. After a long march down the field, the Rattlers scored. Charlie fought back, and Joel was good on a field goal. Riverside was ahead 21 to 16 going into the fourth quarter.

I saw Luke sitting by himself. He didn't look very happy. Maybe he'd realized what his personal vendetta was costing the whole team.

The fourth quarter started out with a fumble by our team. But somehow we held them to an attempted field goal, which they missed. After that, Charlie stirred up our offense, fighting doggedly, slowly covering the ground, tenaciously clinging to the ball.

His determination inspired the rest of the team. When he was forced to kick, Joel made a super effort and then got great blocking to hold the Rattlers deep in their own end zone.

Then came the break we needed. The Rattler's quarterback was sacked, and he fumbled the ball. There was a pileup, but when the ball was unearthed, it was being held tightly by Steve Gory, a freshman who was only put in because Joe McFadden had twisted his ankle on the play before.

That gave Charlie the ball on the Rattlers' thirty-yard line, and he knew exactly what to do. With one minute left in the game, he grabbed the ball, feinted a throw, and ran for the goal line. The rest of the team formed a wedge around him, and we were in the lead, 22 to 21. The convert was good, and the defense hung tough to keep the score at 23 to 21.

As the gun went to end the game, the stands went crazy. Charlie was hoisted on the shoulders of the team, and all Luke had done by his actions was give Charlie the opportunity to be the hero yet again.

At the dance that night, all the guys were shaking his hand and telling him how great he was, and all the girls were drooling over him. He'd come with Marta, but since Nicole wasn't there, he was free to circulate a bit, so he did. You couldn't really blame him.

Luke wasn't there, but Jamie had come with a couple of girl friends. She danced twice with Charlie, and then with some of the other guys.

I talked mostly to Brandon and Matt and a few others about the game. That's all anybody wanted to talk about.

But it got boring after a while. I saw Marta and told her to let Charlie know I was walking home. I ignored her comment about my being too young to be out this late.

I'd intended to go home, but once outside, I found myself walking toward Luke's. The light in his bedroom window was on, so I rang the doorbell. His mom came to the door.

"Oh, hi, Glen," she said with a lot more enthusiasm that I expected from her son.

"Is Luke here?"

"He's upstairs. Should I call him, or do you want to just go up? You haven't been around for a while."

I wondered if she knew why. Or if she knew her son was acting like a first-class jerk. I like Luke's mom. She's somewhat overweight and always kind of flustered, but she's nice enough. She works at the check-out counter of one of the two grocery stores. I think she watches a lot of TV when she's home—the soap opera type of TV. She seems to tune out of real life. Kind of like she doesn't know how to handle things, so she ignores them. Since I wasn't sure I wanted her around to see Luke's reaction to my visit, I said I'd go up.

Luke's dad grunted from behind his newspaper as I went by.

Upstairs, I knocked on Luke's door. His voice said, "It's open."

I went in.

He was sitting on his bed, but one look at me and he was up, moving toward me. "What do you want, creep?"

Chapter 10

I held my cast out in front for him to see. "I didn't think even you'd hit an unarmed man."

"What do you mean, unarmed?"

"Maybe I mean one-armed. Anyway, I just wanted to talk for a minute."

"What about?" he sneered. "How great your friend Charlie is?" But he didn't come closer.

"How about what an idiot my friend Luke is?"

He took another step toward me, and I backed up against the door. "Come on, Luke, somebody has to tell you what you're doing."

"Yeah, so what am I doing?"

"You're trying to make Charlie look bad, but all you've doing is making yourself look bad. All the kids think you were childish to quit the team because Charlie accused you of dropping a ball on purpose."

"Well, I *did* drop the ball on purpose!"

"That was dumb."

"You didn't think I was dumb before your hero Charlie arrived on the scene."

"Maybe I didn't have anything to compare you to," I said, and then wished I hadn't.

"Thanks." He walked over to look out the window.

"Look, Luke, I don't see why I can't be your friend, too. It's you that's angry. Charlie isn't."

"Oh, sure. I've heard nothing but how wonderful he is till I'm ready to throw up when I hear his name."

"Look, Luke, swallow your pride and go and tell Charlie you're sorry. Do it in front of a couple of kids, and everyone will hear about it, and then nobody will be mad at you any more."

He turned. "Glen, do me a favor. Drop dead."

"I didn't expect you to like the idea. But think about it. You don't want everybody mad at you for the rest of the year."

"I'd rather have that than tell that creep I'm sorry when I'm not. And if you don't want your other arm in a cast, I'd advise you to get out of my room right now." He was walking toward me as he spoke, coming so near I could feel his breath.

"Okay, Luke. But you're wrong." I didn't wait for a reply because I thought he was awfully close to carrying out his threat.

Mrs. Trent sounded sorry I was going so soon.

From behind his paper, Mr. Trent grunted again.

Outside, I took a deep breath. Whatever impulse had urged me to talk to Luke the way I just had was gone, and I felt like an idiot. There was no chance he'd do what I said, and he'd likely twist it around somehow to make me look bad.

But I put it out of my mind. As somebody, probably Shakespeare, said, "What's done is done and cannot be undone." I think he was talking about death at the time, though. There I was back to that!

I groaned. Wasn't there anything pleasant to think about? Christmas was coming. School holidays. But there were a bunch of tests and essays due just before then. Ugh!

The play was going well. The sets were designed and construction started. We should have them finished in time.

I strolled along, thinking about the props I still needed to collect.

We went to church as usual on Sunday. My mind wasn't very awake. I think the sermon was something about being a soldier, but it didn't make much sense. Mr. Reiss talked about being thankful, but I didn't hear more than a few sentences.

At the end, he asked how many of us were planning to go to some youth retreat the next weekend. I had no idea what he was talking about, but Charlie put up his hand and said, "Glen, you're going, too. I signed you up a while ago. I must have forgotten to mention it."

I just stared at him. But when we got outside, I yelled. "What do you mean you signed me up for some retreat! Why! How! And what *is* a youth retreat anyway?"

"I don't know. We're all going to a retreat center for the weekend. We stay in chalets of some sort. There's an indoor pool, hiking trails, horseback riding, rafting, and all kinds of stuff. They'll be kids from other churches there too."

"How much is it?"

"It isn't costing you a dime. I figured after all you've gone through helping me, I owed you one. It's all paid."

I groaned.

"We'll have a great time."

"Is Nicole going?"

"Naturally."

"How about Marta?"

He laughed. "I don't think Marta would fit in."

"And you think *we* will?"

That afternoon, Charlie took Marta to a movie in Stanton. I wasn't anxious to go, so I told him I had too much homework. Unfortunately, it was true.

I really did work on it, with a little encouragement from my mother and a few handfuls of cookies to keep up my strength.

The rest of the week flew by. We were busy every day after school getting the sets and props ready. There were rehearsals nearly every day.

Luke avoided me, but at least he also avoided Charlie and didn't do anything dumb. He and Jamie appeared to have made up.

Thursday, I had my cast taken off. My arm felt really weird—light and unprotected. But it was sure nice to get that cast off. Since it had a number of signatures and stuff on it, I took it home with me.

Matt still had his foot in a cast, but he was hoping to have it off soon. It was now the last reminder of our cave-in.

Friday dawned clear and cold. Mom had packed my clothes, so I just added a few things and carried my duffel bag over to Charlie's car. We'd be leaving straight from school. There were enough cast members going to the retreat that rehearsals had ground to a halt. But I knew the actors were pretty well ready, and of course they could all go over their parts on their own.

Classes dragged on, but at last it was time to go.

We all met in the parking lot, and Charlie amazed me by somehow getting Mr. Reiss to put Nicole and Zoey in our car. I think Mr. Reiss must have decided he liked Charlie or something. But then, who didn't? Other than Luke, of course.

Charlie deftly stowed the girls' suitcases and maneuvered Zoey into the back seat. While Nicole was talking to her brother Paul, Charlie motioned to me and I got the message. Without enthusiasm, I got into the back seat beside Zoey. Nicole had no choice but to sit in front, which she did, but she didn't look thrilled.

Zoey immediately asked if I'd mind helping her with her part in the play, and I relaxed in relief. At least I wasn't going to have to try to talk to her! She handed me her copy, and we went through it with me reading the other parts and her giving her lines. We were about to start the third act when she suddenly said, "Glen, I had no idea you could read this well. Why didn't you try out for the play?"

There had been a steady hum of conversation from the front seat—mostly from Charlie—but just then it was quiet.

Charlie turned his head a bit. "What's that? Did you say Glen should be in the play?"

"Well, he certainly can read well," Zoey replied.

I'm sure my face was red. I said, "I don't act. Do you want to finish this?"

Zoey laughed. "Okay, Glen, but you can't keep fooling us forever, you know."

I read her cue, so she stopped talking and started reciting. Charlie and Nicole continued to talk, but I couldn't hear what they were saying.

After we'd driven for about an hour and a half, we found a Burger King and picked up some hamburgers and milkshakes.

When we got back to the car, Charlie suggested I drive so he and Nicole could work on their lines. She looked as if she wanted to say something, but she didn't. So they got in the back seat and Zoey and I got in the front.

I concentrated on driving and Zoey found a radio station that played classical music. That's not my kind, but whatever was on sounded okay. It was some kind of piano concerto by Mozart. Actually, it was a lot better than I'd have expected.

Zoey made the occasional comment on the scenery and I said intelligent things like "Yeah" and "Uh-huh" and the like, and the time passed.

In the back seat, Nicole and Charlie were working on the play.

Zoey gave directions, and we found the place easily. The camp was used year round because it had been winterized. There was an indoor pool plus a rec room with a fireplace and Ping-Pong tables and shuffleboard. Outside there were horseshoes, tetherball, frisbee golf, a baseball diamond, nature trails, horses, a beach area with boats and canoes, and a volleyball net. And there appeared to be ski and skidoo trails, skating, and tobogganing for winter. Not bad at all.

At Charlie's insistence, we carried the girls' suitcases to the chalet they'd be staying in, and then took our own to our chalet.

Each chalet had two bedrooms with two double beds in each, and a pull-out sofa and chairs that made into single beds so you could sleep four more in the combined living room-kitchenette. So it held twelve altogether. Mr. Reiss was there, along with Ted, Andy, Derek, and five other guys I recognized from the youth group. Nicole's younger brother, Paul was there, too.

Mr. Reiss was beaming. Our church had filled two chalets by itself. That was a great turnout, and he was immensely proud of us for making the retreat a priority.

Charlie and I put our sleeping bags on one of the double beds. Derek and Andy had the other. We did a bit of unpacking and then got ready for the first meeting at eight-thirty.

My mom had packed a few clothes items I had no recollection of seeing before—like new pants and a couple of new sports shirts. When I said something about them, Charlie laughed and said he'd helped her pick them out when I was busy working on the scenery one day after school, and if I didn't wear them, I'd hurt his feelings.

I couldn't think of a single reply except "traitor," but he laughed and told me to hurry up. He capped it by reminding me to comb my hair. Since I'd just taken off my T-shirt, I threw it at him.

He ducked and ran out of the room.

When I emerged with my new clothes on, Ted told me how sharp I looked. That was something I'd never heard before.

A bunch of us left the chalet and headed over to the main building where there were a ton of kids. I guess they'd come from a fairly wide area.

After we'd waited a few minutes, the girls appeared and we all sat together in a couple of rows. Charlie again did some tricky maneuvering, ending up next to Nicole, with Zoey and me on her other side.

A music group sang a couple of fast-paced songs; an older man told us how happy he was we were there; a young woman led us in singing a couple of songs; and then a Chinese guy who looked about thirty talked about how hard it was to be a teenager in today's fast-changing world. That was one talk I could relate to.

I looked to see if Charlie was enjoying it, and saw him reach over to take Nicole's hand in his. I watched out of the corner of my eye, but Nicole didn't seem to mind. Charlie's hand continued to hold hers. I tried to concentrate on the speaker, but it was hard. So Charlie was going to win, after all!

The session ended. As we got up to leave, I saw that Nicole's hand was now holding her purse.

Charlie winked at me.

I heard him ask her to go for a walk, but she said she was too tired tonight.

Charlie said, "Tomorrow, then."

As she left, he came over to me, a big grin on his face. "Well, what do you think?"

"Your plan seems to be working."

"You don't have to sound surprised. I could write a book on how to make it with girls. Maybe I will, someday. Let's go play Ping-Pong."

We went to the rec room, and it wasn't long before Charlie was in a close game with a guy from another church. The other guy apparently had a reputation as an expert, so of course that got Charlie going. He won three games to two, and they promised to have a rematch the next day.

Next, we got drinks out of a vending machine and joined a small group of guys and girls from a couple of other churches. They all sat around and talked, only it wasn't exactly what I'd have expected. They were talking about praying for stuff and what they'd read in the Bible lately, and how God was leading them. Even Charlie didn't have much to say, so we both listened. They seemed to believe that God actually cared about every part of their lives and even spoke to them. Weird.

As Charlie and I walked back to our chalet, he shook his head. "Boy, I thought I'd seen some nuts in the city. But they were nothing compared to these guys. If I didn't know better, I'd say they were all high on something."

I spoke quietly, "Do you think the kids from home believe all that?"

"I don't know. Maybe some of them. But not as vocally, at least."

"What about Nicole? After all, her dad is a minister."

"She'd be just the type to believe it. But don't worry, I'll soon get her straightened out."

He wasn't as confident the next day. There was a prayer time at eight a.m., which only some of the kids attended. Paul and two other young guys went over with Mr. Reiss. The rest of us showed up at eight-thirty for breakfast.

The kids who'd been praying were a bit late, and sure enough, the people from last night were with them. So were Nicole and Zoey and Darlene. Nicole was talking to a particularly good-looking guy. She even sat beside him and kept up an animated discussion. I could tell Charlie wasn't amused.

There were workshops scheduled for the morning. We had a choice, so I went with Charlie to one on sexuality, and then one on finances. I guess they were okay, but Charlie was kind of ticked off by how many times the word "responsible" came up. He told me he thought he was pretty responsible now, but if he ever got as responsible as these guys seemed to think he should be, he'd never have any fun again.

Lunch was chili, and it was nearly as good as my mom's. After lunch was free time, and Charlie found some guys who were going to try rafting on a river that ran into the nearby lake. I decided it was a little chilly for me. The water would be like ice if anyone fell in. Anyway, my arm wasn't really ready to do a lot of work. But I persuaded Charlie I'd be fine on my own, so he went.

I ended up wandering over to the stable. My granddad had raised horses, and I'd spent at least part of my summers on his farm until he retired when I was fifteen. I hadn't done much riding lately, and I missed it. Sometimes I thought about getting a horse myself, but it would be expensive, not to mention a lot of trouble to board him and keep him groomed and exercised.

When the stable boy asked if I wanted an easy horse or one for a more experienced rider, I almost said easy, but I caught myself. It occurred to me that riding a horse should be like riding a bike. Once you've done it, you don't forget how.

Sure enough, when I climbed into the saddle, it felt good. And the guy seemed satisfied, because he gave me a map and told me to have fun. The trails were marked and fenced, so I shouldn't run into any trouble.

In the woods, there was no wind and I relaxed and really enjoyed myself. I sensed the horse's willingness to take me where I wanted to go. That meant he recognized that I knew what I was doing. It was a good feeling.

The fallen leaves made a golden path for us. They crackled as we went, and squirrels chattered above as they finished gathering and storing their supplies of nuts. In the sky overhead, I caught occasional glimpses of geese and crows flying in groups. It was great to be alive!

But as I thought that, my mind filled with sorrow for Mr. Jackman and his family. And I thought again of God. It's strange how many different things people believe. Some think there is no God at all and we're just an accident. Others believe there is a God, but that he's not able to help us much, or doesn't care. Then there are some, like those guys last night, and Mr. Reiss, and Nicole and her family, who seem to think God cares about everything you do—even brushing your teeth. You'd think if there really is a God, he'd find some way to let us know for sure.

A horse whinnied nearby and I realized I'd been going pretty slow and a later rider must have caught up. I moved a bit to one side so whoever it was could pass, but the horse came up and stopped, and then I saw the rider was Nicole.

"Hi, Glen. I didn't know you ride."

"Uh, yeah. At least sort of. I used to." As usual, I was showing my intelligence.

"I took riding lessons before we moved to Wallace, but I haven't had much chance to ride here except out at Zoey's."

"Oh, yeah. I guess she does live on a farm, doesn't she?" The path here was wide enough for two, so we rode together now, in no hurry.

"Yes," she said. "They have some quarter horses."

"Oh? I guess maybe I'd heard that."

"Are you enjoying yourself here?"

"Uh, yeah. I am right now, anyway."

"Because of my company or the horse's?" she teased.

I looked around. "Where's Zoey?"

"In the pool. It's heated. And she gets to ride horses a lot."

"Oh." There was a long pause. I grinned. "Aren't you going to ask me where Charlie is?"

She stopped smiling. "I know where he is. A bunch of them went rafting."

"Yeah, they're crazy."

We came up to a meadow just then, and without speaking we both let the horses go. They were more than willing, so we galloped along for several minutes before we again reached woods. Nicole's hair was blown all over, and her cheeks were rosy and eyes sparkling. If Charlie saw her like this, he'd never give up.

"That was fun," she said.

I nodded.

We rode in silence for a while, both of us enjoying the outdoors and the sounds of the horses.

"Nicole," I said, not wanting to break the silence, but really wanting to know her answer. "You believe in God, don't you?"

"Yes," she said quietly.

"Why?"

"Why?" she echoed.

"Maybe it's a dumb question. But I was thinking how some people do and some don't, and I just wondered what makes the difference. Why do you believe and somebody else doesn't?"

We rode on for a few minutes before she answered. "It's not a dumb question. It just sort of surprised me. I guess I believe for several reasons. One is that my parents believe in God and they've always taught me about him. Another is that I can see him in his creation—like these woods or these horses. It's a lot easier for me to believe that an intelligent God made them than it is to believe that they're accidents. Or that I'm an accident myself. Someone very wise had to make us, Glen. Look at all the intricate parts in us. And scientists are always discovering more amazing things."

"Yeah," I said. "It does seem hard to believe that everything in the world is an accident. But how do you know God's still around? What if he just got it going and then he took off or died or something?"

"The Bible tells us he's eternal. He has no beginning or end. He answers prayers, too. And—I just know he's there."

We were coming up to the stableyard, so I said a quick, "Thanks," and led the way in. She'd given me some things to think over, but I didn't want to talk about it in front of anyone else.

I dismounted and held her horse for her. We gave the horses to the stable boy and thanked him, and then we walked toward the chalets.

"Are you going swimming now?" I asked her.

She shook her head. "I think I want some hot chocolate. It's getting cold out here."

"There's a snack bar at the rec hall."

We walked toward it, and I asked for two hot chocolates. I discovered I'd left my money in my other pants, so Nicole paid for both of us.

We sat down near the fireplace. There was a small fire going. I put a couple of logs on, and it blazed up.

A few other kids were around, but none I knew. Nicole asked me something about one of the props she needed in the play, so we talked about the play for a while. Then a guy I hadn't seen before came up behind Nicole and covered her eyes with his hands. He whispered something.

She'd flinched when he first touched her, and pulled away a bit, but after he spoke, she smiled. "Brad!" she exclaimed. "It's so good to see you!"

He laughed. "You haven't seen me yet!"

He came around her chair and she gave him a hug, then held him out at arm's length, "Well, let me have a look. Oh, no, not a mustache! And you've grown another couple of inches! Just how big do you think you need to get?"

"And look at you! Even prettier than when I last saw you. Looks like the Lord has been good to both of us."

I sat there wondering how I could slip quietly away and also wondering if Charlie knew how much competition there was around here.

Just then, Nicole said, "Brad, I'd like you to meet a friend of mine." He came over to my chair and, since he was towering above me, I stood up. He still had a good five or six inches on me.

"This is Glen Sauten. Glen, Brad is my cousin. I haven't seen him since last Christmas."

Brad held out his hand and I followed suit. His handshake was firm and warm. He pulled out a chair and sat down at our table.

I started to make an excuse to leave, but he urged me to stay, so I did. It turned out he was in Bible college and was planning to be a pastor.

I'd never met anyone like him before. He was somehow bold and gentle at the same time. At least that's the impression I got. He was quite willing to talk about what he'd been doing, both good and bad, but his attitude was that everything he'd done that was good had been done by God, but all the mistakes had been his.

We were still there when a large group arrived, led by Charlie. They were cold and wet, but boisterous. The rafting had apparently been a great success.

Charlie walked straight over to where we were sitting, completely ignored Brad and me, grabbed a chair from a nearby table, and sat down next to Nicole. "Here's my girl," he said loudly enough for every person in the place to hear. "Hi, honey, did you miss me? You should have come. It was great."

Chapter 11

Nicole stared at Charlie. Her mouth opened but no words came out.

Brad, however, held out his hand. "Hi," he said, "I'm Nicole's cousin, Brad Hewlitson. I don't think we've met."

"You're Nicole's cousin?"

"That's right."

Charlie held out his hand and the two shook.

Nicole finally found her voice. "Charlie?" She said his name quietly, tentatively.

"Yeah, babe?"

"So how long have you two known each other," Brad asked, obviously interested in this guy who called Nicole "honey" and "babe."

I, on the other hand, was not interested. I'd gladly have disappeared if I'd been brave enough to get up and walk away.

"Charlie," Nicole said again, her voice wavering a little.

"I moved to Wallace just before school started this fall. My dad's the new doctor there."

"Charlie," Nicole said for a third time, her voice a bit louder and stronger now.

Charlie leaned toward her and put one hand on her knee. "Yeah, sweetie?"

Nicole jumped up as if she'd had an electric shock, and her chair flew out behind her. She said, "I—you—" Then she ran out of the room.

"I wonder what got into her?" Brad said.

"No idea." Charlie actually looked puzzled. "I'd better make sure she's okay."

He walked out.

I looked over at Brad. His forehead was furrowed and his eyebrows were drawn together as if he was thinking hard. I wanted to get out of there before he asked me anything about Charlie and Nicole, so I too jumped up, said, "Well, see you later," and hurried back to my chalet.

I thought Charlie might be there—that line about seeing if Nicole was okay had to be phony—but the place was empty except for a couple of the younger guys, who were reading comics.

I decided since I was there I might as well change for dinner. My jeans had a rather horsey smell.

I put on the second shirt Charlie had chosen for me and stood for a minute looking at myself in the mirror. I wasn't *that* bad-looking. Maybe I *should* comb my hair more often. Or do what my sister had suggested and get it styled. Brad looked like he took care of his hair.

I looked at the shirt. It was okay, but not really me. More Charlie.

But then, I'd never spent any time thinking about what I should wear. Mom still chose my clothes, and I just put on anything that looked half decent. Here I was graduating from high school in seven months! Maybe it was time I took control of a few things. After all, it was *my* life.

Speaking of taking control, as I was thinking, Charlie came in. "Well, what do you think?" he said with a smile.

I spun to face him. "I think you're nuts!"

"You don't think that was a smart move?" His smile faded and he looked hurt.

"I think you're crazy. Nicole doesn't go for that stuff."

"What kind of stuff?"

"Being called "honey" and "babe" and "sweetie." Especially when you've never even dated her! I don't know what you were thinking."

"Look, I've tried being polite and all that. It didn't work. So maybe what's needed is the good old he-man stuff. So I'm through asking and I'm going to start telling."

"Charlie, she ran out of the room."

"She was overcome. Wanted to grab me and kiss me, but not in front of everyone, so she ran out."

I stared at him, wondering if he was living in the same world as me.

He changed for dinner, taking time to make sure his pants were creased properly and every hair was in place and stuff like that. I talked to Paul and some of his friends while I waited.

In the dining room, Charlie looked for Nicole, but she was surrounded by Zoey and Darlene and a bunch of other girls. So he and I sat down with some of the guys he'd been rafting with.

I was so surprised by how good the roast chicken dinner we had was that I went and found the head cook and told him it was amazing how he could cook so well for such a big number of kids. He seemed to be really pleased by my saying that, and I realized maybe I should tell people more often that I appreciated what they'd done. Maybe I should start with my mom and dad.

After dinner, we moved to the chapel. Charlie tried to get to Nicole, but he was prevented again by the large group of girls around her. So we found seats near the back.

We did a lot of singing that night, and one of the guys who'd been out rafting sang a song called "He's Alive." It was about somebody dying and coming back to life and what his friends thought. The song was pretty good, and so was the guy who sang it.

Then a girl who looked about thirteen did a ventriloquism act that was hilarious.

Finally, Nicole's cousin Brad got up. He was just like he'd been that afternoon. Very low key. He told the story about how he'd grown up and what he'd done and how Jesus Christ had changed him. He said he used to be shy and tongue-tied and scared of anything new. He seemed so confident now that it was hard to believe him. But he said the trick was that he was not *self*-confident, but *God*-confident. He said something about there being nothing that God and he together couldn't handle.

When he was finished, a couple of people prayed, and then a number of kids went forward to do what they called rededicating their lives to God. I felt kind of embarrassed and I think Charlie did, too. We slipped out and went to a side room where drinks and food were set out. We weren't the only ones getting snacks, but I felt somehow like we didn't really belong there.

I'd seen Nicole go forward, along with several other kids from the church.

Charlie complained that the whole weekend was crazy, but the rafting had been worth it. The only problem was that he hadn't managed to spend much time with Nicole. I told him I'd gone riding, but I didn't mention meeting Nicole. I figured he'd ask me what we talked about, and I thought he might laugh.

We didn't see Nicole again that night. She must have gone straight to her chalet instead of coming for a snack.

Brad was there though. He came over to us and started asking Charlie questions about where he'd lived before and the sports he played and what he planned to do next year. It was a pretty thorough interrogation, though done in a friendly manner. But as I sat there listening, it was obvious to me that Brad was really checking Charlie out. I wondered what, if anything, Nicole had said to her cousin.

Charlie dutifully answered questions without any apparent impatience. However, he complained to me afterwards that he felt he was getting the third degree. "But anything for Nicole," he said.

Sunday was pretty dull. There was an early prayer time, which we skipped. We ended up going for a walk, but it wasn't much fun. He wasn't impressed with nature, and spent most of the time complaining that Nicole seemed to be avoiding him. We finally went back and got Cokes and I helped him go over his lines in the play.

At eleven, there was a church service. Brad spoke again, and again he impressed me. He talked about how God had led him all his life and why he knew God wanted him to be a pastor.

Afterward, there was a wiener and marshmallow roast and some singing. I enjoyed that.

Charlie finally managed to get to Nicole. He toasted a marshmallow and, holding the stick in front of himself, pressed through the group around her.

"Here, Nicole. I made this just the way you like it."

"No thanks, Charlie. It was nice of you, but I'm full." She turned away to talk to one of the other girls.

"I'd like it, Charlie," said Zoey. He had no choice but to give it to her. By the time she was finished getting it off the stick, Nicole had disappeared.

When he'd sat back down beside me, I said, "I think she's avoiding you. Must be something you said."

He glared at me, and I quickly got out of range.

Shortly after that, some kids started giving what they called their testimonies, which seemed to be stories of what God was doing with them.

Charlie dragged me off. "I've had about all of that sob stuff that I can hack. You know, I'm not sure any girl is worth all this."

I nodded. We went back to the room and talked about the play, and then he got into where he was going to take Nicole on their first actual date.

We left the retreat center for home at about three-thirty. This time Charlie got stuck taking a couple of Paul's friends. He was furious, but he managed to keep from blowing up in front of people.

Nicole and Zoey went with Mr. Reiss.

Brad came over to say good-bye. His last words were, "I'll be praying for you both."

On the drive home, Charlie barely spoke. The two younger guys in the back seat seemed to be in awe of him because of his football skills, so they also said very little.

When they did speak, it was to rehash some of the great football plays Charlie had made. He began to loosen up and talk to them about football. By the time we stopped to grab some food, he was in a good mood again.

The first part of the week flew by with preparations for the play, and Thanksgiving took up the rest of the week. My family was all home, so I saw little of Charlie or anybody else.

The following two weeks were the same. The play was all anyone had time for. Luke may have been avoiding both Charlie and me, but I had no time to worry about him.

The play was on Thursday and Friday nights, and it went well. Charlie did a superb job, as did Nicole and the others. Marta wasn't bad. Zoey, however, as the confused Miss Prism, was the hit of the play. She was really amazing. Props had a minor flurry when the cucumber sandwiches went missing the first night. One of the stagehands thought they were a snack. But we found a peanut butter sandwich from somebody's lunch, and covered up.

Charlie cornered Nicole right after the final curtain on Friday night. He stood in front of her as she was leaving the stage.

I was standing nearby with a table in my arms and them in my way, so I had no choice but to listen.

"You were great again," he said. "But what else is new?"

She moved to go around him but he stepped in front of her, blocking her path.

"I think we should go out for dinner tomorrow night to celebrate," he said. "How about I pick you up at six o'clock?"

"I'm sorry. I can't make it."

"So, should I come later—seven?"

"No, I can't make it."

She made another sideways move and again he stepped in front of her. It was like a one on one slow-motion football play. "Come on, Nicole. Give it up. You know I'm crazy about you. So give me a break."

Zoey had been on the opposite side of the stage in the midst of a small group of people from the production crew and other cast members who were no doubt telling her how great she was. Now she came over. "Oh, there you are, Nicole. Hi, Charlie. Nicole, let's get out of these costumes so we can breathe. Can you believe women used to dress like this?" She came up beside Charlie and sort of ran interference as Nicole ducked by him.

But once she was in the clear, Nicole stopped. She was dressed in a long gown that would have been worn in the 1890s, and heavily made-up to look like a lady in her forties, so it was sort of funny hearing her voice come out in its normal tones. "Charlie, I just don't understand you. Why are you so persistent in asking me to go out with you when everyone in the school knows you're dating Marta?"

Charlie blinked once, but he rallied quickly. "I've gone out with Marta a few times, but we're nothing more than friends—plain friends. She's not my girlfriend at all. If you'll agree to go out with me, I'll never go out with her again. I'll never even speak to her again. Hey, I only started dating her in the first place because nothing I said or did seemed to reach you. I thought if you saw me with Marta you'd notice me and get jealous! So what do you say? Dinner tomorrow? And Marta's history. I'll never even look at another girl again!"

"No thanks," said Nicole. "If Marta still wants you, she's welcome to you." She hurried toward the change room.

Zoey smiled at Charlie. "You were great! You must have had a lot of practice." She followed Nicole out.

I set down the table and made like I was busy gathering some of the props that had to be returned to people right away.

Charlie stomped off to change.

Mom and Dad had come to the play, so I went home with them and that way avoided having to listen to Charlie complain.

As we drove out of the school parking lot, I saw Marta and Charlie come out of the front door. He had his arm around her and they were laughing. Maybe he'd get over Nicole one of these days. And hopefully Marta would never find out what Charlie had said to Nicole.

I didn't see him Saturday because I went out of town with Mom and Dad to visit my sister Carrie and her new baby. But he picked me up for church Sunday morning as usual. He didn't say too much then, but after we'd had lunch at my house—his parents were both busy—we went for a drive.

I was a little nervous driving with him; he kept shoving his right foot down for emphasis, and since his right foot was on the gas pedal, we kept speeding up.

"I don't get it! I've never had a girl refuse to go out with me before! Oh, sure, I've had a few refuse at first.

But they always came around." He hit the steering wheel and stepped on the gas. "What's wrong with her anyway? And who's she going to go out with? Luke?" Another hit and stomp and we sped up more. "She turned him down. She turned everybody down and then she goes out with Derek Palmer!" We sped up more. "Why? What's he got that I don't? Nothing! Absolutely nothing! The girl is insane." More speed and this time he hit the wheel with both hands.

He seemed to be waiting for me to respond so I said, "Yeah, it sure is puzzling."

"Puzzling? It's ridiculous. She's got to be out of her mind."

"Yeah."

"Is that all you can say?" More speed.

"Well, I don't know what she's thinking. Maybe she just plain doesn't like you."

"Everybody likes me!" He hit the wheel again.

"Well, Luke doesn't."

"Who cares about Luke! And anyway, he doesn't like me because I played quarterback. What does that have to do with Nicole?"

"I don't know. Maybe she really likes Luke and so she won't let herself like you because he doesn't."

"Glen." We slowed down a little.

"Yeah?"

"Have you ever had any reason to think she likes Luke?"

"No."

"Did she date Luke when he asked her?"

"No."

"So is that a reasonable reason?"

"No."

"So why are you wasting my time talking about Luke?"

"You said everybody likes you."

"Glen." We slowed down a little more.

"Yeah."

"Could you try to say something helpful for a change?"

"I'll try."

"Or else don't say anything."

"You've got it."

There was a long pause. Charlie slowed down to a somewhat reasonable speed and I relaxed a bit. "Do you think Zoey knows why Nicole won't date me?" he said suddenly.

"Probably."

"Would she tell us?"

"I doubt it. If you asked her, she'd just tell Nicole and Nicole would likely get mad because you were talking to Zoey about her."

There was another long silence.

Then a glimmer of an idea came to me. "Paul might know."

"Paul?"

"Her younger brother. He might know. Maybe you could ask him sort of on the side so he wouldn't realize what you were asking. Maybe he wouldn't tell Nicole."

Charlie didn't answer right away, but all of a sudden his foot stomped on the gas again. "Yes!" he exploded. "Yes! That's a terrific idea, Glen. Her brother should know how she thinks. And he might talk to another guy. That's great."

"Yeah, it could work. You should talk to him the first chance you get."

"Didn't you spend some time with him while we were at the retreat?"

How Charlie talked me into asking Paul, I'll never know. But he did. I knew that Paul was one of the kids who helped in the school library after classes on Mondays. He was alone in the back room putting covers on new books when I went in.

"Hi," I said.

"Hi."

"You look busy."

"Yeah. Guess so."

"You like doing this?"

"It's okay."

"I did it a few times when I was younger. I must have been more ambitious back then." I sat on the edge of a desk. I'd already realized this wasn't going to be quite as easy as I'd thought. "Uh, Nicole's in my class."

"Yeah, I know." He continued to put covers on without looking at me.

"She doesn't date very many people, does she?"

"I dunno."

"I mean she only dates a couple of guys."

"I guess so."

I wished I was any place in the universe but here. "Uh, my friend would like to date her."

He shrugged. "Well, tell him to ask her."

"He has."

"So what do you want?" He finally looked up at me.

"Well, she won't date him and she won't even tell him why not."

"Who's your friend?"

"Charlie Thornton."

"Oh, him."

"Yeah. Do you know why Nicole won't date him?"

He had a funny look on his face. "Maybe she doesn't like him."

"Every other girl in the school does."

"Well, *she* might not."

"She hasn't said anything to you? Given you a reason *why* she doesn't like him?"

He shook his head.

"Could there be any another reason?"

"Well, maybe Mom and Dad won't let her."

"Why wouldn't your parents let her date Charlie?"

"Well, all I know is Mom and Dad get the final say as to who we can date."

"But—your parents seem to liked Charlie."

"Yeah." He shrugged, looking anywhere in the room except at me. Even I could tell he was wishing I'd get lost.

But I'd learned too much to quit. "I don't get you. What would make your parents not let Nicole date Charlie?"

"Well, lots of things."

I really felt lost. "They've always been friendly toward him at the church."

"Yeah, but—well, there's more to it than that."

"What more?"

"Uh, look, I'm supposed to be working. If Charlie wants to know, why doesn't he ask Nicole? I've got to get these covers on." He grabbed a book and pointedly started to get a cover ready for it.

I knew he wasn't going to tell me any more, so I left, not sure whether I was further ahead or not. Anyway, I'd done my best.

I hoped Paul wouldn't tell Nicole about my asking him. If he did, Nicole would think I was some kind of idiot, asking dumb questions about her for Charlie.

Oh, well, it really didn't matter what she thought of me.

I reported back to Charlie.

He was as perplexed as I was. "I don't get it. I'm sure they like me. They're always friendly. They had us over for lunch."

"Maybe it's because you go to movies and dances and stuff. Nicole doesn't. Maybe—maybe it's got something to do with what Brad and the others at the retreat were talking about. Something about letting God control you. And praying. They talked a lot about praying."

"Well, I think I've done a pretty good job of controlling my own life up till now, and I have no intention of letting anybody else, including God—if there is a God, which I seriously doubt—take over. As for praying to some invisible guy who likely doesn't even exist, not in this lifetime! So they're going to have to accept me the way I am."

We had a major history project to work on, so we didn't talk about it any more.

Christmas was approaching, and the teachers seemed to want to see how much work they could get out of us before the break.

The youth group's party was coming, too, and Charlie, exasperated, had repeatedly asked Nicole, but to no avail.

"I didn't even try to get her to go to the school dance," he complained. "Why won't she go to the church party with me?"

The following Tuesday, some things happened that changed everything.

First, when we got to our lockers Marta was there. She was wearing another all-black outfit with enormous silver-and-black earrings and dark green lipstick and nail polish. She wasn't smiling.

"So, Charlie Thornton. I learned last night that the whole time you've been dating me, it was to make Nicole jealous. Anything you'd like to say before I tell you exactly what I think of you?"

"I—er—you can't believe—"

"Oh, I believe it all right. I think you're the biggest jerk I've ever met. And you *will* pay for this, believe me."

She turned and walked away.

Charlie tried to laugh it off. "It's not as if she's the only girl in this hick town," he said.

Fortunately the bell rang and I didn't have to respond.

We got through classes okay, but Jamie came running up to us just as Charlie and I were going to his car. "Glen, wait! I need to talk to you. Luke's done something really stupid."

I groaned. "What now?"

"He put a note in Nicole's math book. I don't know what it says, but it's something about Charlie. I think

Marta gave him the idea." Jamie glared at Charlie. "You really shouldn't use people, you know."

Ignoring Charlie's exclamation of protest, she went on. "I don't care about Charlie, but I don't think Nicole needs this. And I don't like to see Luke make a fool of himself—or Marta make a fool of him. I'm sure Nicole hasn't seen the note yet. Can you go to her house and get the note before she reads it?"

She seemed to think I was some kind of genius.

"No," I said.

Charlie cut in before Jamie could say any more. His voice was smooth and cold. "Sure we can. I don't like being made a fool of either, so we'll get the note. Thank you very much for the warning."

A few minutes later, we were parked a block from the Grants' house, and Charlie was telling me how we were going to case the place.

Actually, luck was very definitely on our side. As we started up the block, we saw Pastor Grant walking over to the church after saying good-bye to Mrs. Grant, who had the younger kids in the car. We heard her tell him not to forget that Paul would be late, and she said something about the dentist, and they were gone. That only left Nicole to worry about.

Charlie found a place for me to hide near the house and told me to go in as soon as Nicole came out. Then he ran back to the car. I waited about two minutes; then Nicole came out and hurried over to the church.

I figured with my luck she'd have locked the front door, but it opened easily and I slipped inside. Cautiously, I moved down the hall. Something in my mind was telling me you could go to jail for breaking into a house. How on earth had I let Charlie talk me into this? Then I remembered the note and what Jamie had said about Nicole not needing to get involved in Luke and Charlie's quarrel. It was true.

I'd checked the kitchen and was wondering where else the book could be when the phone rang. What should I do? But after four rings it stopped. I walked back into the hall. Just then I heard voices. It sounded as though people were coming to the front of the house! It sounded like Mr. Grant and Nicole!

Realizing I was standing right next to a door, I opened it and went inside the room. It was Pastor Grant's study. I heard the front door open and the sound of their voices as they came into the house. They seemed to be coming toward me! In desperation, I looked for a place to hide. There was another door behind me. I opened it and ducked inside a small closet seconds before Nicole and her dad walked into the den. I felt like a complete fool, but it was too late.

Chapter 12

One thing my mom and dad managed to teach me is that it's not polite to eavesdrop. But situated as I was, I really didn't see what else I could do. I tried to close my ears, but...

"Nicole, let me get this straight," Mr. Grant's voice said. "You want to go to the Christmas party with some-body?" He sounded puzzled.

I didn't hear Nicole's answer, but it was obviously yes.

"I don't understand why you're telling me this. Do you want help in asking him?"

"No, of course not," Nicole said. "It's just that there's a problem."

Her dad sounded amused. "Don't you think he'll go with you?"

"It isn't that, Dad. It's just—well—" She paused, then hurriedly got out the next words. "It's just that the boy I want to ask isn't from our church. I mean he's not from *any* church. He's not a Christian."

Mr. Grant's voice lost its tone of amusement. "You know our rules, Nicole. We don't want you going out with anyone who isn't a Christian. I thought you agreed."

"I do agree, I guess. But—well, as far as I know there are only three Christian boys close to my age in this town."

"Can't you go with one of them?"

"Andy is going with Darlene. Zoey is going with Ted."

"That leaves Derek. You've been out with him before and never complained."

"What use is complaining? It was him or nobody."

There was a long pause, and then she said, "Dad, it isn't that I want to go out with a *lot* of non-Christians. I just want to go out with one. Who knows—maybe he'll become a Christian soon."

"What's wrong with Derek that suddenly makes you want to start looking elsewhere?"

"Oh, Dad, you don't understand. Derek talks like a Christian, and I suppose he is one, but the boy I want to go out with is worth ten of him!"

In my mind I compared Charlie and Derek. Nicole had understated. Derek was a loud-mouthed bore. Charlie was worth twenty of him.

Pastor Grant's voice broke into my comparisons. "I assume this paragon you want to date is one of the two who've been coming around lately, Charlie Thornton and Glen Sauten?"

"Yes."

I squirmed, wondering how on earth I'd let Charlie get me into this mess. Were they never going to leave? I tried to move my right leg—it was so cramped I didn't think I could stay still any longer.

Then a miracle happened. The doorbell rang.

I heard steps moving away. The study was quiet. There were voices at the front door—Pastor Grant's and Charlie's. Good old Charlie. He must have realized what had happened and was giving me a chance to escape.

I carefully opened the door and peered out. All clear. I extricated myself from the closet. Limping, I moved across the room so I could see out the door. All three were standing in the front hallway. Pastor Grant and Nicole had their backs to me. Charlie was laughing and saying something about the youth group party.

Ignoring the needles in my leg, I slipped out of the study, across the hall, and into the kitchen. I hurried on tiptoe across the room and silently slithered out the back door. When it was closed, I took a deep breath. Then, as if I could feel Pastor Grant's eyes on me, I raced down the steps, across the yard, and into the back lane. My leg hurt until the circulation got going, but I could have yelled for joy just to be out of there.

I slowed down at the corner. The only problem was that Charlie may not have seen me, so he might not know I was out. I turned the corner and started walking toward Grants' house. Did I dare go to the front door? What if they'd seen me?

My heart was in my throat as I rang the doorbell. If they knew—

Nicole opened the door. I couldn't help noticing that she didn't look very happy.

I tried to smile. It must have been hard for her to have her dad say she couldn't date Charlie when she wanted to. At least now we knew the reason. But I still wasn't clear on what this business of being a Christian meant. We'd been going to the church for what seemed like months!

She smiled. "Hi, Glen. Are you looking for Charlie?"

It didn't sound as though I'd been spotted. I relaxed. "Yeah, sort of," I said.

"Come on in."

We walked toward the family room. I tried to think of something to say to cheer her up. What was it Mom had said once? Girls like to know they look nice. I did my best. "Uh, your hair looks good like that."

She glanced up at me and smiled. "Why, thanks, Glen."

I didn't know what else to say, so I didn't say anything. Anyway, we were in the family room and Pastor Grant was telling Charlie something about some carol singing that was coming up.

I half-listened. I was wondering if I should tell Charlie what I'd overheard—about Nicole wanting to date him and her dad not letting her. I was also wondering what he'd say when he found out I hadn't been able to get the letter.

An idea popped into my head. I turned to Nicole. "By the way, did you bring your math book home? We had some homework, didn't we?"

"Yes."

"I forgot to write it down. Do you know what it was?"

I think she gave me a funny look, but she said for me to wait and she'd get her book. She came back with it a minute or two later. I was sure she'd find the letter right away and then—well, who knew what would happen! I held my breath while she opened the book.

Charlie and Pastor Grant were deep in conversation about the caroling. But I should have known Charlie would be alert. He suddenly said, "Nicole, what do you think about my idea?"

Nicole glanced up to find Charlie and Pastor Grant both looking at her. She hadn't been listening at all, so Charlie explained his idea.

Seizing my chance and mumbling something about finding the page, I took the book from her.

The letter was inside the back cover. It was just an ordinary lined page folded in half—not something easy to hide.

For once I used my head. I took the pen out of my shirt and started writing on the folded note.

Math homework, page 97, questions

When Nicole came back, I was waiting for her to tell me which problems to do. I wrote the numbers down and then casually folded the paper smaller and stuffed it into my shirt pocket. I looked up to find Charlie's eyes on me and a big smile on his face. He told Pastor Grant that it was time we went, and we got out of there.

Once outside, we hurried down the street to where Charlie had parked his car, and sank onto the cushions. For a couple of seconds, neither of us spoke. Then Charlie started laughing and slapped me on the shoulder and laughed some more. "Oh, man. I never thought you had it in you!"

"Me, neither. And if you ever try to talk me into doing something like this again, I'm taking you straight to the loony bin. If you knew what I went through in there when I heard Pastor Grant and Nicole come in! Oh, brother!"

"So what did you do?"

"Well, I'd just barely got in and I was trying to figure out where she'd have put her homework. I thought maybe the kitchen, but no luck. I was still there when the phone rang—"

"That was me," Charlie said. "But no one answered. I guess she'd already gone out of the house. That's what happened. I was going to get her out for longer than a couple of minutes."

"How?" I asked.

"Never mind. What happened next?"

"Just after the phone stopped ringing, I heard them coming and ducked into a closet in the study, and not a second too soon, either! I thought maybe they'd forgotten something and would go out again. But, instead, they came right into the study and started talking. I don't want to think what would have happened if you hadn't rung the doorbell."

Charlie laughed some more. He thought it was great. Then he sobered. "I take it the paper you had was the one?"

I reached into my pocket and brought it out. We both read it, and I had to admire Luke's invention, even though I sure didn't think much of his using Nicole to get at Charlie. I wondered if that part was Marta's idea.

Dearest Nicole,

You seem to believe that my desire to be with you is simply an ordinary boy/girl kind of thing. I want very much to assure you that it's nothing of the kind.

Rather, my feelings for you are such that I'm suffering daily. I wake in the morning with your name on my lips. All day long, I cherish every glimpse of you. I dream of you all through the night. I can't eat. I can't sleep. Please end this suffering.

I don't wish to be just a friend. My feelings for you are far stronger than that. The next time I call at your house it will be to ask your father for your hand in marriage.

Yours eternally,

Charles Thornton

When he'd finished reading it, Charlie swore. "I'm going to wring his neck. I'm going to—"

"Charlie?"

"The nerve of that guy! I save his rotten life and this is the thanks I get. Believe me, he's going to pay for this!"

"He did get Jamie to tell us, Charlie. Maybe he was sorry about it. And Nicole never saw it. At least, I don't think she did. Otherwise it wouldn't have still been there."

"You don't think she read it?"

"If she'd read it, why would she leave it in the book for me to find?"

"Yeah. But just because Luke got cold feet and had Jamie tell us about it doesn't mean he isn't going to regret this. It was just pure luck we got it away from her. Boy, what a sap I'd have looked with Nicole's dad expecting me to ask if I could marry her. That—"

"Charlie?" I said again.

"What?"

"Why do you want to date Nicole?"

"What a dumb question. Why do you think?"

I didn't say anything.

Charlie laughed. "Hey, I forgot. You're the one who isn't into dating, aren't you?"

"Yeah, I guess."

Charlie turned the key and the motor sprang to life. "Well, Glen, remind me one of these days to tell you a little story about the birds and the bees."

I didn't say anything. The thought of what I'd done had suddenly overwhelmed me. If Pastor Grant had caught me in the house, he could have had me arrested!

I sank further into the seat. Why I'd let Charlie talk me into anything so dumb—!

But that wasn't exactly true. I mean, I hadn't really done it for Charlie. He could have talked his way through it, told them how Luke had written it and all. No, the fact was I'd done it because I didn't want Luke to be caught being so dumb. And because I didn't want Nicole to get hurt. If Luke wanted to dislike Charlie, okay, but he had no need to drag Nicole into the middle.

I sat in silence till we got home, me getting madder at Luke, and Charlie no doubt trying to think of some way to get even. But when I asked him what he was going to do, he just laughed and told me not to worry about it.

"And, hey," he said as I started to walk over to my house, "thanks a lot." His eyebrows went up. "You know, you really surprised me with that little play about the math questions. You used your head there."

I grinned. "Not really. In fact, if you don't need that letter, I could use it. I was telling the truth about forgetting to copy down the assignment this morning."

Charlie burst out laughing, slapped me on the back, gave me the letter, and went whistling into his house.

I carefully put the paper in my pocket and went home. I had some thinking to do. Somehow, what had started as a fun thing—seeing Charlie try to get Nicole to date him—had gone sour. I was tired of it. Especially now that I knew there was more involved—that Nicole really did want to go out with Charlie, but her dad wouldn't let her.

I realized I hadn't told Charlie what I'd overheard. And I still didn't understand the part about her not being able to date him because he wasn't a Christian. I had to try to figure that one out. There must be something in all those sermons and classes that I'd missed. Of course, I miss a lot of stuff.

Mom was making dinner when I got home and dropped my stuff on the kitchen table.

"Oh, there you are, Glen. I was wondering if you'd be home in time. Mrs. Pearson wants to know if you'll go and carry some things up from her basement. I said you'd be glad to help. You've got about half an hour before dinner."

"Yeah, okay." I stood there.

"Glen?"

"Yeah?"

"Are you going?"

"Where?"

"To Mrs. Pearson's. Don't you ever listen?"

"Yeah. Mrs. Pearson's. Okay." I turned to go.

"You do remember where she lives, don't you?" Mom sounded almost sarcastic.

"Yeah." I paused and looked back. "Mom, what's a Christian?"

"What?"

"A Christian. If you said somebody was one, what would they be?"

"I see why you get low marks on grammar."

"Never mind that. You know what I mean, don't you?"

She shrugged. "Well, I guess a Christian is somebody who does the right things. A civilized person. It's the opposite from a—a cannibal or something. Why? Is this for your homework?"

"It's got to mean more than that."

"Well, look it up on your computer." She pushed me toward the door. "But do it later. You've barely got time to help Mrs. Pearson before dinner. Hurry!"

I walked down to Mrs. Pearson's house, just three doors from ours. She's a nice lady who used to give me cookies all the time when I was a little kid. I guess she gave them to all the little kids in the area. She's been a widow for about five years. Mr. Pearson was a big man, kind of fat and jolly. Whenever anyone mentioned Santa Claus, I always think of him. I hadn't seen too much of Mrs. Pearson lately. In the winter, I shovel her walk and do a lot of errands for her. But I'd only seen her a few times this summer and fall when I did a bit of yard work.

The door opened almost as soon as I knocked, and Mrs. Pearson hurried me inside. She's a fairly stout lady with gray hair and bifocal glasses. She always wears a dress and a checkered apron, and her face is set in a permanent smile. "Why, Glen—" she gave me a hug "—thanks so much for coming over. I know you boys are busy all the time with school and sports and everything, so I appreciate your helping me out."

"Oh, that's okay. What can I do?"

"It's just that I've got some boxes down in the basement that I want to get rid of. I decided a while ago that

I simply had to go through my whole house and throw out things I don't need." She led the way downstairs. "You know how one tends to accumulate. After living for nearly 75 years, you can accumulate a lot!" She laughed and I did, too.

"Anyway, I got some boxes from Mr. Marshall at the grocery store and got busy filling them. There, you see." She pointed to a group of boxes in the middle of the basement floor. "These boxes all go in the trash. There are three of them. The other five I thought I'd give to the church ladies' group. They try to collect things to give to people in need at Christmas."

"Church?"

"The one I go to. You went with me sometimes when you were younger. Remember? I took you to Sunday school."

"Oh, yeah. I sort of remember."

"You seemed to like it. But your family was so busy doing things that you didn't get to come much. I guess you don't go at all now."

"Well, I do sometimes, only—" I was embarrassed "—I go to a different one, the Community Evangelical Church."

"Oh, yes. Pastor Grant's the minister there, isn't he?" I nodded.

"He's a good man, too. His outlook isn't very broad, maybe, but that's all right. We can't all be the same."

"Mrs. Pearson, do you know what a Christian is?"

"Well, what a question! A Christian is someone who goes to church, Glen. And who tries to live a good life."

"A good life?"

"Well, you know, helping people. Being a good person. Like carrying boxes for an old lady." She laughed.

I did, too, and then I realized I'd better hurry or I'd be late for dinner. I carried the three boxes upstairs and put them out for the garbage truck in the morning. I said I'd take the other boxes over to her church whenever it was a good time and I could get the car, and she thanked me. She tried to give me a couple of dollars, but I said she didn't need to and went home.

Mom and Dad were ready to eat. Mom had made a meat loaf with baked potatoes and other stuff, and I suddenly realized I was starving. I guess I'd used up a lot of energy, what with the happenings at the Grants' and all.

After dinner, I took my books to my bedroom and got out my homework. I had a report to write for English. Not my idea of fun, but I got some words out. Teachers get a lot madder when you don't do anything than when you slap something together. I'd done the chemistry assignment during a study period, so all I had left to do were the math questions. There was a test in physics coming up, but I wasn't in the mood for studying. Turned out I couldn't concentrate on the math, either.

The fact was I hadn't been satisfied by what my mom or Mrs. Pearson said a Christian was. It seemed to me Charlie fit both their definitions. He didn't break laws—well, except maybe for speeding sometimes, and he was civilized, and he'd helped people—saved a few lives, even. He'd been going to the Grants' church since he got here. So there must be something more in Pastor Grant's mind.

What had Nicole said? Something about only three boys her age being Christians? Who had she said? Andy,

Derek, and Ted. Only she'd said something else. About Derek not really acting like one and how Charlie was worth ten of him even though he wasn't a Christian. So there had to be more to it than how you acted.

I remembered a little of what Mr. Reiss had said Halloween night about people wearing disguises. I also remembered what Brad had said about having God in your life and letting him control you. But I couldn't quite put it all together. It was a bit like a jigsaw puzzle, and I wasn't sure I had all the pieces yet. Maybe Pastor Grant had said something at church about it, but I'd never bothered listening much.

Charlie had paid attention more than me, so maybe he knew more. But for some reason I was reluctant to tell him what I'd overheard. I guess I'd enjoyed seeing him so frustrated by Nicole's always turning him down. Now that I knew Nicole was unhappy, it wasn't funny any more.

I pulled out the letter Luke had written. It wasn't funny, either. I wondered how Charlie would get even.

I did my best to concentrate on chemistry, but at last I shut the book. I found Dad in the living room watching a rerun of "M*A*S*H*."

"Dad, could I use the car for a little while?"

He looked up. "What for?"

The question grated. Charlie had his own car and never seemed to have to tell his parents where he was going.

"I just want to go out," I said with a note of anger.

"Then I guess the answer is no."

I stared at him and clenched my teeth.

"If you can't tell me where you're going, you don't get the car. You know that, Glen."

"I'm not a little kid."

"If you were, you'd never get the car."

I felt frustrated, but somehow I managed to control myself.

"I want to go over to Luke's. There's something I need to talk to him about."

"Schoolwork?"

Did he have to know everything?

"Sort of. Well, it's just—he did something really dumb and I want to talk to him about it."

"What kind of something?"

I decided to tell him the truth. "He wrote a stupid letter and signed Charlie's name to it. He put it into Nicole's math book. I got hold of it before she did, but now Charlie's mad at Luke. Luke just can't stand Charlie and I— well, I don't know what to do about it."

"Because you want to be friends with both?"

"Yeah. I mean Luke's always been my best friend till lately. And Charlie's okay. But they hate each other."

"And I take it Nicole is involved?"

"Not really. It's just that Charlie's been trying to date her, only she won't go out with him. Luke found out and put a—well, a mushy letter in her math book. Only then he wished he hadn't, and he got Jamie to tell me. So I got it out before Nicole read it. But now Charlie's mad at Luke and says he'll get even. I don't know if I should do something or not."

I'd been wandering around the room, but now I sank into a chair. "Any suggestions?"

"Sounds like a good tangle. And you're caught in the middle. Why do they hate each other?"

"I don't think Charlie hates Luke. Luke's just jealous."

"Jealousy can be pretty powerful."

"Yeah."

"Well, why don't you drive over and have a talk with him. You know, when you get consumed by jealousy, the only person you really hurt is yourself. Try to tell him that. But watch it. Don't come back with a black eye."

I laughed. Somehow, I felt better. Now if only Luke would be home and ready to listen to reason.

Luke's mom said he was in his room doing homework and I should go on up. I knocked on his door and heard a mumble, so I went in.

He was on his computer, but when he saw me he got up and flung himself on the bed.

I shut the door, tossed some clothes on the floor, and sat on his computer chair.

"So?" he said brusquely.

"So what?"

"Did she read it?"

"I don't think so."

"Did Charlie get it?"

"I did. He read it, though."

"So he knows."

"Yeah."

"What d'ya want now?"

"Charlie said he'd get even."

"Big deal."

"I'm just warning you."

"Yeah. First you let Charlie see the letter; then you tell me he's gonna get even. You some kind of dumbass?"

"Guess so."

"Okay, you've told me. You can get lost now."

I didn't move.

"I said get lost."

"How long have we been best friends, Luke?"

"We aren't."

"We used to be."

"Maybe."

"Until this summer."

"Yeah, when Charlie showed up. So you like him better than me. That's your choice."

"No, it was when you started dating Jamie. You didn't have time for anybody else. I started going around with Charlie because you were busy."

"Oh, sure."

"You know that's true, Luke."

He didn't answer.

"You still spending all your time with Jamie?"

"None of your business."

"I don't care. I mean, it's up to you how you spend your time. Only it seems to me you've changed. You didn't do dumb things before. At least not as dumb as what you've been doing lately."

"Thanks a lot."

"I mean it, Luke. You did stupid things. We both did. But now you're drinking and starting fights. This letter to Nicole—you had no business involving her."

"I told you about it, didn't I? Anyway, it was Marta's idea."

He got up. "I had Jamie let you know so you could get it back!"

"Yeah. I guess that means you're not really mean. Just acting like it. The thing is, Luke, you're not bothering Charlie. He thinks it's all a big joke."

Luke glared at me.

"Look, we've always been best friends, and, believe it or not, I still want to be. That's why I came over. If you want to spend most of your time with Jamie, okay. And if I want to have Charlie as a friend, too, there's nothing wrong with that."

Luke flexed his arm. "Yeah, well you can forget it. I'm not your friend and I never will be again. And if I were you, I'd—"

"Shut up! I'm not done. I came over here to tell you you're acting like a two-year-old. You're jealous of Charlie, but all you're doing is letting it get to you. You're gonna get ulcers or something! So Charlie's a better quarterback! You could have worked at it and taken his job away. No, you could only sulk about it! That's all you've done. Feel sorry for yourself."

Chapter 13

I saw he was ready to hit me, so I ducked. He swung and just missed clobbering his computer monitor. I went past him and opened the door, then turned to face him.

He stood glaring at me.

"You're only hurting yourself, Luke. Believe it or not, I don't want to see you make a fool of yourself. I still happen to like you."

I stepped into the hall, shut the door, and went downstairs. I was breathing fast, but I was very pleased with myself. I don't remember ever talking to anyone like that before, but it felt good. It especially felt good that I'd managed to do it without getting clobbered.

At home, Dad asked how I'd done and I showed him I didn't have a black eye. He laughed.

I went to my computer and Googled "Christian meaning." There was a whole bunch of stuff, most of which seemed to deal with Christ. Different groups seemed to have different definitions, but in general it seemed to mean a person whose life conformed to Christ's teaching. There was something about gentleness, humility and service. And I found what Mom had said about not being a savage. I was no further ahead. Unless? I checked the word "Christ," but that didn't help much either. Christ was the Messiah, who had something to do with Jesus, and it was also a title of Jesus and part of his name. Okay, I'd heard of Jesus Christ—mostly when guys were swearing. And I knew he was in the Bible. Pastor Grant had mentioned him in his sermons. So had Mr. Reiss.

It seemed to me the Bible might hold the answers I needed. Maybe if I could get hold of a Bible, I could find out what a Christian was. Then I could tell Charlie, and he could do whatever it was to be one, and he'd be able to go out with Nicole!

For some reason, I wasn't quite as happy as I should have been. True, I'd solved the problem of why she wouldn't date him. But—? But what?

As I lay on the bed, it was as if someone suddenly switched on a light in my brain. The truth was I didn't *want* Charlie to go out with Nicole! The fun had been that she'd never seemed interested in him. Now that I knew she really was—!

What was wrong with me anyway? Charlie was one of my best friends and Nicole was—well, just the nicest girl in town. Why shouldn't they date?

Because I didn't want them to, that was why! I didn't even want to think about her being with him. It was okay for Marta and Sophie—for any of the other girls—but not for Nicole. She was too good for Charlie. Too good for anybody I could think of—Derek or Andy or any of them.

But I'd heard her tell her dad she wanted to date Charlie, hadn't I? Yeah, but that's what he'd been working so hard at—making her want to go out with him. Suddenly, I had to know how he really felt. Was it just because he wanted to date every pretty girl, or was it because he really liked Nicole?

I grabbed my cell phone.

Charlie answered on the second ring. "Hi, Glen, what's up?"

"You busy?"

"Just finishing up my homework. After that I was thinking about popping over to the Diner. Want to come?"

"Yeah."

"Okay. Half an hour."

"See you."

I ran upstairs determined to get my math homework done so I didn't have to lie to Mom.

Somehow, I managed to answer the questions. I have no idea if the answers were right though. I saw it was time and went downstairs.

Mom and Dad were sitting in the living room reading the paper and talking.

"Charlie and I are going for a Coke. Okay?"

"Homework done?" Mom asked.

"Yeah," I said with a twinge of guilt.

"Okay. Not late, though."

"Nope. See you later." I grabbed my jacket and ran across the street. Charlie was backing the car out of the garage. I got in.

"Charlie, I want to talk to you for a couple of minutes."

He laughed, "You worried about what I'm going to do to Luke?"

I'd forgotten about that. "Some. At least—well, I went over and talked to him. I wish you two could be friends."

Charlie looked thoughtful. "It seems to me he's the one who's always causing problems."

"You irritate him."

"That's up to him."

"Yeah, I know. But sometimes I think you kind of enjoy getting his goat. Like cutting in on him and Jamie at the dance."

"If he wants to act like a little kid, that's up to him."

"Well, you don't make it any easier," I said.

He laughed. "You remind me of a bantam rooster getting ready to defend his territory."

I couldn't help smiling. "Charlie, I just—"

"You just don't like people fighting. Okay, how's this? I won't try to get even. As long as Luke doesn't start anything else, I'll leave him alone. I'll even say hello next time I see him. How's that?" He grinned that wide grin, eyes laughing.

"That's sounds great," I said with relief. What a guy! He really was as nice as he seemed. Now if I could only get Luke to go along.

"Was that it?" Charlie asked, still grinning.

"Huh?"

"Was that all you wanted to talk about?"

Then I remembered the real reason I'd phoned him. I shifted in the seat.

"Well, actually, there was something else."

"Okay, shoot. I'm getting thirsty."

He'd driven past the Diner and we were out of town on a side road. I stared at the fields for a minute. Charlie slowed down and made a left into a dead end. He turned the car around to face town and put it into park.

"Well?" he said as he flung his arm over the back of the seat and shifted to look at me.

I swallowed. "Well, it's just—I wondered…"

Charlie was clearly amused, "Keep going."

"Well, I was just—just wondering…"

"Glen, you're going to have to finish one of your sentences. What do you need? Money? Help with your homework? A date? What?"

"Nicole," I blurted out. "What do you want with her?"

He stared at me. "What are you talking about?"

"Why do you want to date her? You seem to go for girls like Marta and Sophie. Nicole isn't like them at all. You've been doing all kinds of things to make her interested in you, but I don't think you really enjoy them. Like church and all."

"You blind?"

"What do you mean?"

"My boy, Nicole Grant is a knockout. Capital K. She's by far the best-looking thing in this hick town. Likely in this part of the country. She's gorgeous."

"You mean that's *it*?"

"Isn't that enough?"

"You've been trying like mad to date a girl you've got nothing in common with, just because she's pretty?"

"Why the heck did you think I wanted to date her?"

"I guess I thought you liked her."

"I *do* like her."

"Because she's pretty."

"Not pretty. Beautiful."

Light dawned once more. "And out of reach. That's all it is. She's the only girl around here who didn't fall for your line. And you can't have that. The best girl has to be yours."

Charlie didn't speak for a minute. Finally, he flashed a rueful grin. "Oh, come on, Glen, you know me better than that. You make me sound like some kind of a machine."

"No, Charlie. Just a plain teenager with problems like the rest of us. Only I didn't realize it until now."

For the first time, Charlie looked away.

"It's not your fault, I guess, Charlie. Maybe a lot of it is mine. I was too self-centered and just plain lazy to care. It's kind of weird. I've been thinking about it lately. In fact, I've been doing a lot of thinking lately. I guess I've been sitting back watching life go by. I got a kick out of seeing you go after Nicole—and just watching you, period."

I was on a roll now. "But that isn't all. I've spent my whole life watching from the sidelines. Like in school. Just enough to get by. When my parents and teachers wanted me to work harder, I've always eased my way around them. Until everybody knew I was just good old Glen. Nobody that really counts. A little spaced out— foggy—just ignore him—everybody does. I was so dumb that I tried to help you get the only girl I've ever cared about. Pretty funny, huh?"

Charlie started to say something, but I ignored him. "The point is, Charlie, it's over. Rip Van Winkle has awakened at last. I guess most of it is thanks to you. You and Luke. Somehow, you two woke me up. So I owe you a lot of thanks. If there's anything I can reasonably do to repay you, let me know. But there's one thing I'm not doing, and that's helping you try to con the—the nicest person I know. If you really cared about her it would be different. But you don't! So I'm warning you. Marta probably still likes you. Sophie. Peggy. And a bunch of other girls. You've got your pick of them. But stay away from Nicole, or you'll answer to me!"

I got out of the car. I had my phone in my pocket, but I decided not to use it to call my dad. It was probably going to take me an hour to walk back to my house, but I didn't care. If I couldn't walk that far at my age, it was time I learned.

I'd gone about a hundred paces before I heard the motor start. Particles of dirt bit into my face as Charlie roared past. I watched the dust trail swirl toward town. He was mad. He had reason to be. But I wasn't sorry for what I'd said.

By the time I reached town, it was late and I was dead tired. I was more than a little worried, too. I'd had lots of time to think, and to realize what a mess I was in. Luke and Charlie were both mad at me now. And Nicole! I'd told Charlie to stay away from her even though I knew she liked him. So I'd messed things up for her, too.

Of course, Charlie would ignore what I'd said, so it wouldn't make any difference. But Charlie didn't know Pastor Grant wouldn't let her date anybody who wasn't a Christian.

And I still didn't even know what that meant. I had to find out.

I got home at last. The house was dark. I found the key in the mail box and let myself in.

After all that walking I was thirsty, so I went to the kitchen. I drank a couple of glasses of water and then sat down with a glass of milk and a handful of cookies.

Dad came into the room. "It's after eleven."

"Yeah, I know."

"You said you wouldn't be long."

"Yeah."

"What's wrong?"

"Oh, nothing. I just told off my two best friends. So now, instead of hating each other, they both hate me."

"I see." He poured himself a glass of milk, got a cookie, and sat down across from me. "Maybe it'll look brighter after a good sleep."

"Yeah, I guess." We ate for a minute in silence. "Dad?"

"Yes, Glen?"

"What do you think of me?"

"What do I think of you?"

"Yeah. As a person, I mean."

He coughed. "Well, you're a teenager, which means you haven't really finished growing up yet. But—well, I like you. I mean besides your being my son and all."

"Yeah, but look at Charlie. He's got his own car and nobody tells him what he has to do."

"No, you don't have your own car. But it's not because we love you any less than Charlie's parents love him. It's just that they have their—beliefs, I guess—and we have ours. We don't honestly feel you need a car. Besides, none of our kids had a car before they finished high school."

"I could have bought one with my money."

"And it would have taken a lot of your money. Money you need to go to college."

"That's another thing! You always say I'm going to college. But I don't know why. I don't even know what I want to do. And my marks aren't very good."

"Are they as good as they could be, Glen? Can you honestly answer that?"

I looked in his eyes. Were my marks as good as they could be? I'd scraped through for as long as I could remember. "I don't know."

"Why don't you do an experiment?"

"Like what?"

"When's your next test?"

"Monday. Physics."

"Okay. That gives you five days. Do you think you can spare five days of your life to find out something?"

"I guess so. What?"

"I say you could get an A on that test."

"If I studied?"

"That's right. *Really* studied."

"Did I ever get As when I was a kid?"

"A few. Till it started to be work. The thing is, Glen, you've never cared much for hard work."

"You really think I could get an A if I worked?"

"How does fifty bucks sound?"

"Huh?"

"If you work real hard, and miss getting an A, I'll give you fifty bucks."

"Yeah, but—"

"Sounds like a bad deal for me, doesn't it? But you asked me what I thought of you as a person, Glen. I'm saying you've got too much integrity to rip me off. I also think, for what it's worth, that down the line you're going to be someone who is trustworthy and honest and, yes, even courageous—a son any father could be proud of. You're getting awfully close to growing up. Anyway—" he went over to the drawer where Mom keeps her emergency money "—here's the money. Give it back when you get the A." He threw down two twenties and a ten and went back to bed.

Coming on top of everything else today, what my father said left me stunned.

I'd always known he loved me and all that, but I'd also always thought he regarded me as—well, something to tolerate. Like, after five good kids, I'd been given to him as a sort of bum deal.

But now—why, he'd really sounded as though he genuinely liked me! As though he was actually glad I was his kid!

And the money! What a crazy deal. He'd give me fifty bucks if I *didn't* get an A! Me, who hadn't had an A since, well, for all I knew, kindergarten. I started to laugh. He was nuts.

I put the money in my pocket and the empty glasses in the sink. Then I turned off the lights, brushed my teeth, threw my clothes in the hamper, and went to bed. The last thing I remember thinking was how Mr. Berezowski's face would look as he marked my paper and found I'd got an A. It would be almost worth it just for that!

The next morning, I was so beat that Mom almost had to drag me out of bed. But she succeeded in the end—she always does. I ate some cereal and toast, quickly grabbed my books, and ran out. I'd realized that Charlie wouldn't be waiting for me, so I started toward school by myself.

It seemed funny to be walking alone. Of course, I'd often done it before Charlie moved in. I noticed Randy Winheart ahead of me. He's a year or so younger. I hadn't noticed him much lately, but now I caught up and asked him how his classes were going. He seemed surprised, but soon we were talking about school and stuff.

Charlie was already in his seat. I sat down in front of him and looked over at Luke. He was at Jamie's desk, talking to her in a low voice. When Mr. Jackman came in, Luke went to his own seat, but he didn't look in my direction. Jamie did, but she didn't smile.

I got through the day somehow. A few teachers asked me questions, but they were used to me by now, so when I didn't know the answer they just asked someone else. No big deal. Just the same dumb Glen.

I remembered what my dad had said. I wondered if he really meant it or if he'd just been trying to make me feel good. Last night, I'd thought he meant it.

During study hall, which was the last period of the day, I sat and watched Nicole. She was one row over and two up, which made it easy. She sure was pretty—as beautiful as Charlie had said. But she was more than that. She was—genuine. She didn't giggle and try to impress guys like most of the other girls. I guess she acted older than them. She was smart, too. I bet she hardly ever got a mark that wasn't an A.

And she had something—self-confidence, maybe. You knew she was exactly like she seemed—friendly and— well, just nice. She was even friendly to me. I mean, most girls kind of treat me like I don't count, but she's always nice. Yeah, nice to dumb old Glen.

I surprised myself by the force with which I threw my pen to the floor. I also surprised Mr. Oliva and the other students. I felt my face turning red as they all stared at me—including Nicole. I bent and picked up the pen. Mr. Oliva said something—I think it was a joke—if so, I didn't get it. Nearly everyone laughed, but I didn't. I'd never felt so frustrated in my life. Maybe it was like my dad said. Maybe I was finally growing up. If so, I wished I'd waited a while longer.

The period ended at last. I looked for Luke, but he and Jamie had gone. Charlie was talking to a couple of kids.

I went to my locker and sorted through it. At the bottom of the pile was my physics book. I remembered my dad's challenge, but there didn't seem any way I could get an A. Too much of the year was already gone. Still— the test was only on the last three chapters. And I had until Monday. I added the book to my backpack, shut the locker, and headed home alone.

When I got to my room, I started my homework. I answered some questions about a story in the English book. I'd done most of the chemistry in study hall, so I finished it off quickly. I looked at my physics book. Could I do it? Could I really get an A? Well, there was no time like the present to find out.

I studied most of Wednesday and Thursday nights. Friday, I worked on an English essay that was due Monday. In my usual way, I'd forgotten about it until Miss Carter reminded us.

Saturday, I did some stuff for Mom and then took Mrs. Pearson's boxes over to her church. On the way

home, I picked up some groceries for Mom. I spent the
rest of the day alternating between the essay and physics.
I'd discovered that I had to go back through the first part
of the physics to really understand the chapters we were
being tested on. I didn't think there was much hope for
an A, but I was beginning to think I might squeeze out a
B if Mr. Berezowski stuck to reasonable questions.

Sunday morning I woke up about nine o'clock. I
knew that church started at ten. Did I want to go even
though Charlie wasn't dragging me along? It would take
time from studying. Then I remembered that I was still
trying to figure out what Pastor Grant thought a Christian was. I decided to go.

Mom had stopped being surprised at my going to
church. She just fried some eggs and made toast and didn't
comment. "Charlie coming for you?" was all she said.

"Nope. Not this morning."

"Do you want to take the car?" Dad asked from
behind his newspaper.

I'm sure I sounded surprised. "I—yeah, that would be
great."

He handed me the keys and went back to the paper.

I ate breakfast and then drove to the church. I'd never
come without Charlie before, so I was kind of nervous.
But a couple of people said, "Hi," and the usher handed
me a bulletin and showed me to a seat, so it wasn't hard.
Nicole and Zoey were sitting near the front with a couple
of other girls. I saw Charlie come in and sit beside Ted
and Andy.

The service began at last. They sang a song I'd never
heard before, and then there were announcements. Nicole

and her brother Paul sang a duet. It was pretty good. I hadn't heard her sing before.

Finally, they got into the sermon. Pastor Grant was talking about something in the Bible called Romans, but he lost me pretty quickly. It was to do with gifts and the church being a body or something. But he didn't say much about Christians or Jesus Christ.

When it was over, I got out pretty fast. I didn't want to stay for the youth group—not with Charlie there and all. I went out the front door and toward my car. Somebody had parked behind me. I couldn't leave till they did.

I decided it would look dumber for me to sit in the car than to go to the group, so I slowly went back into the building. Nicole was near the door, talking to her youngest sister. She saw me and told her sister to go find their mother. She said, "Hi, Glen."

"Hi."

"Did you give Charlie back his letter?" She turned and went downstairs.

I blinked. That little—! So she *had* read it. I felt my face getting redder and redder. Did she also know I'd been in the house?

I ran after her and caught up at the bottom of the steps. "Nicole!"

She stopped. "Yes?"

"You read it?"

"Yes. But I didn't think it was very funny."

"It wasn't supposed to be funny."

She didn't say anything. Just kind of looked at me.

"Charlie didn't write it. I mean, he didn't even know about it till afterwards."

"Oh. I suppose it was *your* idea of a joke, was it? What's the matter? Did you chicken out at the last minute?"

She hurried into the rest room, but not before I'd seen that she was about to cry.

Chapter 14

She did cry easily. Like if she read a really sad book or something, she couldn't keep a few tears from falling. Even some of our English books. I'd hate to take her to a sad movie. No, I wouldn't. I'd love to take her to a sad movie. She could cry on my shoulder all she wanted.

The thought shook me. Nicole and me. Nicole on a date with me. All of a sudden, I was the one who wanted to cry. I knew how impossible—crazy—it was.

People were passing me in the hallway. Charlie could have reached out and touched me as he went by with a few other kids. He didn't even look at me.

Nicole came out just then and they waited for her. She walked to the youth room with them.

I stood rooted to the floor. I couldn't go to the group now. Nicole actually thought *I* had written that lousy letter. Was that the kind of person she thought I was?

Everyone had gone into the various rooms. A few of them had given me some funny looks.

I made my feet work. I went up the stairs. I'd just go for a walk until it was over and the cars were moved.

I was going toward the front door when I noticed someone come out of a room. It was Pastor Grant. He stopped and looked at me.

"Hello, Glen," he said.

"Hello, sir." I wondered if Nicole had told him about finding the letter.

"Anything wrong, Glen? If you're worried about being late—"

"No sir. It isn't that."

"Something else then?"

My collar felt tight. I'd come here hoping to find out what a Christian was. Did I dare ask him? Why not? This might be my big chance. "Well, uh, I was just… Well, you see, I… Well, what is a Christian, anyway?"

"What is a Christian?"

"Yeah. See, I looked it up on the Internet, but it didn't tell me enough. Something about following the teachings of Jesus Christ, but I don't know what his teachings are. Mrs. Pearson thought it meant going to church and helping people, but I kind of thought it must be more than that. Is it?"

"Glen, I'll tell you what. Instead of standing out in the hall, why don't we sit down in my office? Here, you go in and sit down and I'll be right back."

I noticed the books in his hand. "You were going somewhere. You lead one of the groups, don't you?"

"Don't worry about that. I'll be back in two minutes. Have a chair."

I went in and sat down, feeling guilty for being in his way. But it was nice of him to take the time.

He was back before I expected. He shut the door and sat behind his desk and leaned forward. "Now, Glen, you asked me what a Christian is. Do you know who Jesus Christ is?"

"A man who lived a long time ago?"

"That's right. A man who lived for a while, and who died. But, unlike us, he came back to life."

"You mean he wasn't really dead?"

"Oh, no. He was dead all right. But he didn't stay dead."

"Oh, I see. I mean, I don't really. How could he be really dead and come back to life?"

"Well, it goes back quite a way. Glen, let me ask you something. Have you ever sinned? I mean ever done anything wrong? Anything you felt bad about after?"

I thought about sneaking into his house. "Yes, I have."

"Well, you aren't alone. There isn't a person who's lived who hasn't done something wrong. And usually it's lots of things. You know, if you were to live seventy years and only do one thing wrong each week, that would be three thousand six hundred and forty wrong things, or sins. Most of us do more than one a day."

"Yeah."

"Do you know what that makes us?"

"No," I said after a second.

"It makes us sinners."

"Uh, okay."

"How many times would you have to murder someone to be a murderer?"

"Just once."

"Well, it takes one sin to make us sinners, too."

I didn't say anything, because I had no idea what he was getting at.

"Now, to get back to what a Christian is. Did you know that God made us—this world and everything in it?"

I nodded. "Yeah, I guess so."

"Do you think your life on this earth is all that there is Glen? Do you believe there's a heaven?"

I shrugged. "I dunno. I mean, I don't know much about that stuff."

"Well, let me tell you, there *is* a heaven. No doubt about it. That's where God lives. And the exciting thing is that that's where you could go when you die. Now I know"—he picked up a pen and held it between his hands—"I know that you're young and you don't think about death. But, Glen, it happens. People of all ages die. A car accident. A brain tumor. Cancr. You never know."

He let the pen drop. It clattered onto the desk. "So what happens? How do you know you'll go to heaven?"

He had my interest. Because I'd thought about dying. Back in that cave-in, I'd known I wasn't ready to die. That had shaken me up. Then later, when I'd heard about Mr. Jackman's son and realized how hard it is to prevent death—

"Well, you know, Glen, God has a sort of exam for those who want to go into heaven. But his passing grade is pretty high. It's one hundred percent. Only people who have no sin are allowed to go there."

I remembered Mr. Reiss saying something similar once. It hadn't made sense to me then and it didn't now, either. "But you just said everybody sins! So it means that nobody can go there!"

"That's right. And God knew that. But because he loves us in spite of our faults, he made another way. He declared that the blood of a completely sinless person who died for the sins of all people could make a way.

Anyone who accepts the sacrifice of that person can enter heaven, because he took their sins on himself."

"But, if nobody could be without any sin, how—?"

"He knew that, too. That's where Jesus Christ comes into the picture, Glen. The Bible tells us that 'God so loved the world that he sent his only begotten son that whoever believes in him shall not perish but shall have eternal life'." He held out his Bible. "That's found here, in John chapter three, verse sixteen. You see, Jesus Christ was the Son of God himself. He came down to earth as a baby and lived as an ordinary man. When he was thirty-three years old, he allowed men to kill him—nailed to a cross for all to laugh at and scorn. But three days later, God brought him back to life in a new body so that all could see that the sacrifice was enough—that God was satisfied. So, now, everyone has the opportunity to accept God's sacrifice and go to Heaven when they die."

"Is that what a Christian is?"

He smiled. "A Christian in the most accurate sense of the word is a person who believes that Jesus Christ was the Son of God and who asks Jesus to take over his life and make him a new person. You see, Glen, the marvelous thing is that we don't have to wait until we're dead to have that eternal life. It starts the moment we accept Jesus Christ as our Savior. The Bible says we're born once, from our mother, but that we can be born again as sons of God. Someone once said that we only exist until we become God's, and then we start to live."

"Are you a—a Christian?"

"Yes, Glen, I am. I have been for a number of years. In fact, my parents were Christians, so I've known about

Jesus all my life. I was seven when I asked him to give me eternal life. My wife was fourteen. Her family weren't Christians then, but she heard about Christ at a camp."

"I guess Nicole's one, too."

"Yes. She asked Jesus to come into her life when she was about four." He was looking at me steadily as he talked. "What do you think, Glen? Would you like to know more?"

"I guess so. I've never heard all this before. I mean, I guess I sort of knew about Christmas being about the birth of Christ, but I never really… It's all kind of strange."

"Yes, I guess in a way, it is." He picked up a small book. "Take this. It's the Gospel of John. It's just one of the many books that are found in the Bible. It's a good book for someone who doesn't know a lot about Jesus because it tells about his life and his teaching. When you've read it, come back and talk to me again. Jot down any questions you have, or just put a question mark in the margin. Don't be afraid to write in it. I'll do my best to answer your questions for you."

I took the small book from him and put it into my back pocket as I stood up. "Well," I said, "thanks for taking the time to talk to me. I know you're busy—"

He stood up and held out his hand. I took it rather awkwardly and we shook hands. "Any time, Glen," he said. "I'm never too busy to talk to someone about Jesus Christ." He smiled and I couldn't help smiling back. He reminded me a little of Nicole when he smiled. Like he really meant it.

I went out and found that people were talking in the halls. The time had sure flown.

I didn't see Nicole or Charlie. Which was good. I had a lot to think about.

When I got home from church, Mom had lunch ready. I didn't say much. Mom and Dad asked me if I wanted to drive over to Stanton with them. They were going to visit some friends there. Normally, I'd have gone. Not today.

I read a few chapters in the booklet Pastor Grant had given me. If this stuff was so important, why had I never heard it before. Why didn't they teach it in school? And how come my parents and Mrs. Pearson didn't know it? Or Charlie and Luke?

I put the book down after a while and got out my physics text. The test was tomorrow morning. I forced every other thought out of my mind and concentrated on physics. I kept at it, only stopping now and then to get a snack, until Mom and Dad got home at ten. When Dad asked how I was doing, I gave him a dirty look. He laughed. Mom made us milkshakes, and we went to bed.

I didn't sleep well, though. I had nightmares where Nicole and Luke and Charlie were chasing me through a maze made of different kinds of levers and fulcrums. They were all yelling that they hated me.

Determined that I wouldn't be bothered by the fact that three people in my class hated me, I went to write the physics test. Anyway, Nicole didn't take physics, so I only had to be aware of Luke's and Charlie's presence. Luke was sitting at his desk looking at his textbook; Charlie was joking with a few girls as if he didn't have a care in the world.

I sat down, mentally going through the chapters, wondering if there'd be any easy questions.

Then the test was on. It was weird to glance through the questions and realize that I recognized them all. Normally, I was lucky if I could make sense of more than half. I got busy.

I was on the last question when the period ended. "You can have a couple of minutes to finish," Mr. Berezowski said.

I glanced up and saw that there were only five of us left. Charlie stood up and handed his paper in. He said something to Mr. Berezowski, but I didn't listen. I was busy writing down all I knew about inertia.

"Glen, time's up," Mr. Berezowski said. "It's lunch time."

I wrote the last few words, then put down my pen. Glancing around, I saw that everyone else was gone. I quickly handed him the test. I was usually among the first to finish a test. I'd never been last before.

After lunch, we had English. At the end of the English period, when I handed in my essay, Miss Carter picked it up and looked surprised. It occurred to me that this essay was a lot longer than usual, and on time.

The bell rang and I decided to skip study hall. I'd done enough studying lately. Instead, I went down to the library, found an isolated corner, and got out the Gospel of John.

It was sure different from anything I'd ever read. If it was really true, I'd been missing a lot.

I was nearly at the end when Marta sat down across beside me.

"What class is that for?" she asked.

"No class. I—er—I was just reading it because I wanted to." I quickly closed the little book and stuffed it into my pocket. I was scared stiff she was going to ask for details, but fortunately she had something else on her mind.

"I want to talk to you."

"Well, talk lower then. This is a library and some people are trying to work."

"Tell me the truth."

"About what?"

"Charlie. You're his best friend."

"Was."

"What?"

"I *was* his best friend. Sort of."

"You had a fight?"

"You could say that."

"I thought you were glued together. You always seem to do whatever he wants. And you never argue with him."

"The same could be said of you."

"Is it true he was just using me to make Nicole jealous?"

Why did I have to come to the library instead of going to study hall? "Yes—no—I don't know."

"Do you know anything?"

"I know he wants to date Nicole. But I don't think he was only going with you to make her jealous. I mean, I think he likes you, too. It's just that she refuses to go out with him, so that—"

"Makes him want to go with her even more?"

"Yeah. But if it's something more than a challenge for him, I honestly don't know."

"So what did you two fight about?"

I realized I'd actually been talking to Marta as if we were friends. I looked her over—long black jumper over a black turtleneck sweater, long black boots, purple lips and nails, gobs of black stuff all around her eyes. Scary. "Nothing to do with you." I said, starting to get up.

"He likely found a smarter yes-man."

"Yeah, I guess." I walked away.

The bell rang a second later, so I kept going home.

Once there, I made a peanut butter sandwich. Mom's note said she'd gone shopping. I didn't feel like touching a book after what I'd done the last few days. Normally, I'd have gone to the pool hall or someplace with Charlie. Last year, I'd have tagged along with Luke. Tagging along! That's all I ever did. That and be a yes-man as Marta had said.

Disgusted, I turned on the TV, but that only made me feel worse. There was an old movie on—a western—with a hero and his sidekick. That was me—the sidekick. People either laughing at him or ignoring him.

I shut off the TV. Who was Glen Sauten anyway? And what did he want to be? I guess I'd never really looked at myself before. I'd always been satisfied to exist, to tag along with somebody else, to let other people make the decisions. But so what? I was happy, wasn't I?

No, I wasn't. Not anymore. What was it Charlie had said about girls? That one of these days I'd wake up and realize what I'd been missing? Well, I guess that day had come. The question was—what did I do now? In a way I'd cut loose from both Luke and Charlie: they were both mad at me. I was on my own.

The front door bell rang, interrupting my depressing thoughts. I found Mom there, her arms full of bags.

"Oh, you *are* home. I thought you were. Thanks, Glen. I shouldn't have carried so many things. I could have taken them to the bank and let your dad bring them. Oh, well, they're here now."

"What did you do?" I said as I put several bags on the kitchen table. "Buy the stores out?"

"Not quite," she laughed. "But I did get a couple of new dresses, shoes and a matching purse, a new T-shirt for you, and a few Christmas presents."

"Getting ready, huh?"

"Mm-hmm. Most of the things were on sale." She pulled a blue dress from one of the bags and held it up. "Like it?"

"Yeah, I like the colour. It'll look good on you."

She showed me the other stuff she'd bought and I dutifully said I liked it all—including the T-shirt she'd bought me. It looked kind of orange—rust, according to Mom.

"So, how was the test today?" she asked as she refolded the clothes.

"Not bad."

"Any chance for an A? Your dad told me about the deal."

"Maybe."

"And if not, you get to keep the money?" She shook her head. "I hope he doesn't try too many deals like that at the bank."

We both laughed. Then I peeled the potatoes for her.

After dinner, I forced myself to do homework and I tried extra hard to do a good job. That meant going back in my math book. But some of it still didn't make sense. I finally took the whole mess out to Dad and got him to explain some things. Fortunately, he's good in math, and after he explained the questions to me, they began to make some sense.

It was after ten when Mom brought us each hot chocolate and a piece of pecan pie. "You're both working so hard, I thought you deserved something special." We heartily agreed. Funny, though. Despite the hard work, I'd kind of enjoyed it.

The next day passed about the same as Monday, except I spent the evening reading some history stuff that I'd been putting off. Neither Luke nor Charlie spoke to me or acknowledged my existence in any way. But at least I hadn't noticed them getting at each other, so maybe it was worth it.

Marta was back to being her obnoxious self, as if anyone cared. I just ignored her. I didn't know if Charlie had made up with her or not.

I'd seen Nicole looking at me a couple of times. I wasn't sure what to do there. For some reason, I didn't want to have to explain to her that I hadn't written the note. Anyway, how could I tell her the truth without involving Luke? So, if she wanted to think I'd written it, let her.

We got our physics tests back Wednesday morning. Mr. Berezowski gave me a funny look as he handed me mine. I looked at the mark—93. I looked again. He must have written the numbers backward! But as I checked each question, I discovered that I'd made very few mistakes.

I sat there totally stunned. I'd never dreamed I could actually get an A. It was unreal.

I looked up and saw Mr. Berezowski watching me. He likely thought I'd cheated. But I hadn't! It was really my 93. Maybe it was a fluke, but at least I'd done it once.

I nearly laughed out loud. I had to give back the fifty dollars Dad had bet me. That A had cost me fifty bucks!

I tried to concentrate for the rest of the class, but it was hard. I felt like jumping up and telling the whole school what I'd done. But, of course, I didn't.

When the bell ended, I picked up my books and walked with Brandon to the lunch room. He said he'd got a 62 and how had I done? I was half scared to tell him.

"That bad?" he said.

I showed him my paper.

He stopped dead and stared at me. "That's yours?"

I nodded, grinning.

"Where'd you have the answers?"

I pointed to my head and walked into the lunch room.

He sat down at the nearest table, still staring at me, shaking his head. I couldn't help grinning.

My grin got even wider after lunch when we went to English class. Miss Carter handed back the essays and my paper had a B+ and a "Very good, Glen!" on it. When I looked at her, she smiled back. Usually I was lucky to get a C. B+? Why, that was almost an A! Me? In English?

Brandon and Matt cornered me after school so Brandon could show Matt my physics test. I showed them the essay, too. They were as stunned as I was. "Are you sure you're feeling okay, Glen?" Matt asked. "I think maybe there's an alien in your body."

"No," Brandon said, "it's all the time you spend with Charlie! Some of his brains are rubbing off. Next thing you know, Charlie'll get a C."

I laughed and asked them if they were going for a Coke. After pretending to be afraid to be in my company, they said, "Yes," and we walked downtown.

I stopped in at the bank and gave one of the tellers, Mrs. Robinson, the fifty dollars. I asked her to give it to my dad. Then I ducked out.

Brandon and Matt made me buy, on account of my "good luck." That was okay.

A few minutes later, Luke and Jamie walked in and sat down in the booth behind us. Matt started to call Luke, but I told him to skip it.

"Does he know what you got?"

"No, and he doesn't need to know," I said.

"Do you two have to keep fighting?" Brandon asked.

"Just agreed to disagree," I answered. "Let's talk about something else."

"How come you haven't been with Charlie all week?" Matt asked.

"Come on, you guys."

"Well, you've been with him most of the time since he moved here."

"Yeah. Well, I guess I'm on my own now. Okay?"

"Sure," Brandon said. "You going to the Christmas dance?"

"What dance?"

"The one at the school."

"Oh, that one. No. How about you?"

Brandon's face got red. "I'm taking Linda Rogers."

"Yeah? She's kind of nice." Linda is in the eleventh grade and she's a superb basketball player. I don't think she dates much. I was surprised Brandon would ask her out since he isn't really into sports. I was surprised she'd go with him for the same reason.

Brandon shrugged. "Matt's taking Sally Kent."

"Yeah?" I said, surprised. Sally is in another grade 12 class. She's fairly pretty but very quiet. I wondered if she and Matt would talk at all.

"I thought you might have asked somebody," Brandon said without looking at me. I guess he thought I'd feel bad.

"Nope," I said.

"You still aren't interested in girls?" Brandon asked.

"Nope," I said. "I'm not interested in girls." A half-truth. If he'd said *a* girl, well....

Just then, there was a crash in the booth behind us. We looked around and saw Jamie get up and walk out of the restaurant. I caught a glimpse of her face. She was mad.

A minute later, Luke stood up. Harry came over to see what had broken. He and Luke talked for a minute. Then Luke strode to the door, his face furious.

At that very moment, Charlie walked in. Luke collided with him and yelled, "Watch where you're going!" Then he saw who it was. He stepped back and swung. His fist caught Charlie full on his nose and spun him around.

Charlie went back against the open inside door. But he immediately got clear of it. They stared at each other.

Harry ran over yelling, "Stop! No fighting in here. I'll call the police."

They ignored him. Charlie came in swinging, but Luke ducked and punched him in the stomach. Charlie backed up, then hit Luke hard on the shoulder. Then they were really into it. Charlie knocked Luke off his feet and leaped on top of him. They rolled in front of the door.

Harry grabbed the phone and started yelling for the police to come before his place was wrecked.

Matt and Brandon and I just watched, along with the rest of the people inside and a few who were watching through the glass in the door.

Luke and Charlie were on their feet now, both breathing hard. Charlie's nose was bleeding and Luke had a cut under his left eye. They both had their shirts ripped and they looked like a couple of raging bulls.

Luke charged. Charlie managed to turn sideways and give him a vicious chop on his back. Luke turned and hammered Charlie across the neck. They were both out for blood.

"We'd better stop them," I said.

Brandon and Matt just looked at me.

"Wait a minute." I ran over to Harry and asked if he had a pail. We hurried to the back room and got a couple of big containers, which we filled with ice water. From the sounds, we could tell that the fight was still going strong.

When the buckets were filled, we each took one and hurried back. They were on the floor again, Luke on top, both punching like mad. Brandon and Matt helped us dump the ice water all over the two of them. That cooled them off in a hurry. They broke apart and started swearing at us.

Brandon and Matt held Luke back while Harry and I helped Charlie to his feet. What a sight! They both looked like they'd been stomped on by a herd of cattle.

They were still mad, but by now they were also close to being worn out, so we were able to keep them apart.

I guess the match-up had been pretty even, but if I had to pick a winner, it would be Luke. He seemed to be able to ignore everything except the fact that he'd finally messed up "Charlie's pretty face." Charlie, on the other hand, was spitting mad at Luke, both for starting the fight and for still being alive.

We were wondering what to do next when the police car drove up and Sergeant Crammer and Officer Speck came inside. Crammer has a daughter in our class, and an older girl who used to be best friends with one of my sisters, so it isn't like the police are strangers.

They took a look around and talked to Harry for a minute. When they found out about the water, they laughed and Officer Speck said, "That's using your head." Then he looked Charlie and Luke over and said, "More than I can say for you two."

Luke looked at the floor.

Charlie started yelling, "Arrest that idiot! He started it!"

Some of the kids nodded. A few said they hadn't noticed.

Luke mumbled through his bruised lips, "Sure, I started it. But he asked for it!"

"Okay." Officer Crammer grinned. "I can see you were having a great time. All the same, let's get you to a doctor and then decide whether to lock you up for a few years or not."

They took both of them out and put one in the front and one in the back of the squad car. Crammer got in. Speck came back to the restaurant. "Did any of you actually see what happened?" Brandon and Matt and I nodded. The others said, "No," or "Sort of."

"You three saw it all?" he said to us.

We said we had, so he took our names and asked us to drop by the station and give the desk sergeant our statements. We said we would, and he left. The car drove away.

I hadn't noticed Marta before, but apparently she'd been outisde the door during the fight. Now she came over. "Glen. I didn't know you had it in you. That was just absolutely perfect! Did you see his face?"

I assumed she was referring to Charlie.

"Beautiful!" she said. "Tell him for me that if I was a guy, I'd have doen the same as Luke. And when he goes to get his car, tell him that the flat tires are on me." Still laughing, she went to the counter to join Emily.

I looked around. Most of the crowd had dispersed. Harry was busy mopping up the water. Brandon and Matt had gone back to the booth to finish their Cokes.

I ran outside and found Charlie's car parked a few stores down. Sure enough, it had four flat tires. Man, was he going to be sore.

I smiled. He'd treated Marta badly. Not that I liked her at all. She's a total nuisance. But still, Charlie deserved it.

I went back inside and joined Brandon and Matt. We looked at each other.

Brandon spoke first. "Wow. That was sure a humdinger."

"Yeah." Matt whistled.

I put my chin on my hand. This had been some day. First the marks at school, then the fight between Luke and Charlie, and now Marta's revenge.

And it wasn't over yet. I still had to make a statement to the police about how the fight started. How could I explain that it went back nearly four months, and that it wasn't either one's fault? Or rather, that they were equally to blame? And how serious had Officer Crammer been when he talked about locking them up for a while?

Matt, Brandon, and I slowly walked the three blocks to the station. We went in and told Officer Murphy why we were there.

He got out a paper and said, "Okay, who's first?"

Chapter 15

Brandon nudged me, but I said, "They are," and went over to a chair by the wall. I heard Brandon and Matt tell how it happened—how Luke collided with Charlie and then hit him, and how Charlie hit back. They made all sorts of excuses for Luke, since he was more of a friend than Charlie, but it still came out sounding like it was mostly Luke's fault.

When they were done, they all looked over at me. I got up and said, "See you guys tomorrow. No sense waiting for me. I'll get a ride home with Dad."

So Brandon and Matt left.

"Your version different from theirs?" Officer Murphy asked. I didn't know him. I'd delivered groceries to his house during the summer, though, so I knew his wife a bit. His kids were quite a bit younger than me.

I sat down. "Sort of."

"Okay, let's hear it."

"Well, what they said was true. It's just that they don't know everything."

"And you do?"

"I think so. They're both my best friends. Luke and Charlie, I mean. At least, they used to be."

"So the fight didn't just start today. Is that it?"

"No, sir. It's true Luke's got a pretty quick temper. Only he usually gets over it quickly, too. Charlie's done a lot of things that irritate him. I don't know if he means to or not, but he still does. Will you really put them in jail?"

He smiled. "Well, there was damage done in the restaurant. That'll have to be paid for. They were certainly disturbing the peace, never mind assaulting each other. It might depend on how much trouble they've been in before."

"Luke hasn't. Not with the police, I mean."

"That will help."

"I guess I just wanted you to know it wasn't entirely Luke's fault. It's just—well, Charlie to him is like a red flag to a bull. I told him he's just jealous—but—well, it didn't do much good."

"Okay, Glen, we'll keep it in mind. Say hello to your dad for me."

I walked down to the bank. It was nearly five-thirty and I found Dad locking the door to his office, ready to go home.

"So," he said as we pulled out of his parking spot, "Mrs. Robinson gave me fifty dollars today. She said it was from you."

I'd forgotten all about that. And right now I couldn't work up any enthusiasm. "Yeah," I said.

He looked at me. "What's the matter? Didn't you think you should keep it?"

I tried to sound a little happier. "You said I only got it if I didn't get an A."

"What did you get?"

"93."

"Are you putting me on?"

"Nope."

"Glen, why I—! Glen! Why—that's just great!"

"Watch the road, Dad."

He was both happy and surprised. So he hadn't really expected it.

Mom had dinner ready—lasagna—but I wasn't overly hungry. Dad told her about the test and of course they both had to see it.

So I showed them the essay, too, and they were both just as pleased as could be.

Meanwhile I stared at the lasagna.

"Glen, what's wrong? You should be delighted!" Mom said. "Are you feeling okay?"

"He's just worried we'll expect A's all the time now," Dad said, laughing.

I hadn't thought of that. Likely they would. But I'd worry about that some other time.

"Luke and Charlie are in jail," I said.

They stared at me.

"They had a fight at Harry's. Luke started it. He'd just had an argument with Jamie, and then Charlie walked in and Luke accidentally bumped into him, and when Luke saw who it was, he hit him and there was a fight."

"Was either of them hurt?" Mom asked.

"Not badly," I said. "But they sure looked a mess."

"Did Harry call the police?" Dad asked.

So I told them everything that had happened, down to making my statement at the station.

"I don't blame you for not being hungry, Glen," Mom said. "I wonder if there's anything we can do?"

"I'll phone Jack Trent and see what he's heard," Dad said. But there was no answer at Luke's.

Mom walked into the living room. "There aren't any lights on at Thorntons' house," she said as she came back. "I expect his parents had to go down to the police station to get him."

So we ate some dinner and then I wandered around the house. I tried watching TV, but I was too restless. I dug out my little Gospel of John and tried reading it, but I couldn't make much sense of it. I remembered what Pastor Grant had said about dropping by. Well, even if he wasn't there, the fresh air would do me good.

I told Mom and Dad I was going for a walk. Dad offered me the car keys, but I said I needed some exercise.

I walked past the school and over to the new area where the Grants live beside the church. I didn't see any lights on at the church, so I walked toward the house. Likely he was busy. Anyway, I wasn't brave enough to go to the door. What would I say if Nicole answered it?

I walked past the house. Then I stopped. What kind of chicken was I, anyway? I'd come to see if I could talk to Pastor Grant. Did I expect him to be standing outside waiting for me?

I forced myself to walk up the sidewalk to the front door. I remembered that 93. If I could get an A in Physics, I could ring a door bell!

Nicole opened the door.

"Yes?" she said without a hint of a smile.

"Uh—" I bit my lips "—is—is your dad here?"

"Just a second."

She left me standing there.

In a minute, Pastor Grant came to the door. He was a lot friendlier than his daughter had been. "Come on in, Glen. Did you drop by for that talk?"

I nodded.

"Well, let's go to my study. I have a meeting at eight-thirty, but we should have plenty of time before then."

We sat down in his study. I glanced at the closet door, remembering how cramped I'd been in there.

"So, have you done any reading in the book I gave you?"

I pulled it out. "Yeah, I've read it twice. But I still don't understand a lot of it."

We went through it. I'd put in a lot of question marks, so it took quite a while. It was after eight when we finished, and I knew I hadn't nearly understood everything.

"I guess the key thing, Glen, is that every person has to decide who's going to run his life. Is it going to be you, or is it going to be other people whose leading you follow, or is it going to be God? That's the key question. But what you have to realize is that people make mistakes and God doesn't."

I thought about it. Up until now, I guess I'd let other people run my life: Mom having to tell me everything, doing whatever Luke or the guys did, then Charlie. Only in the past week had I been making my own decisions.

I had two good marks because I'd decided to study. Yeah, but I'd also managed to get everybody mad at me. And I sure didn't feel confident about not making more mistakes.

I coughed. "Mr. Grant, I mean Pastor Grant, I guess it makes the most sense to let God do it. I mean, if he loved us enough to send his son to die for us, and if he knows what he's doing all the time, it only makes sense for us to let him tell us what to do."

"It certainly does, Glen. Would you like to do it right now?"

"You mean—"

"I mean tell him that you want him to forgive you for all the wrong things you've done and come into your life and start making you into a new person."

"Don't I have to be a better person first?"

"No. He loves you exactly as you are right now."

"Then—how do I do it?"

"Just ask him to forgive you and to take over your life."

"Okay." I did what he said. I didn't do it all that well, maybe, but I did it.

Then he prayed for me, that I'd have faith and that I'd grow strong. I felt good. I knew I'd done the right thing.

Pastor Grant was smiling as he hunted through his desk. "You mind reading some more, Glen?"

"No, not if it makes sense."

He laughed. "This will." Then he gave me a couple of little booklets and a complete New Testament. He told me to read the booklets and to start at the beginning of the New Testament with a book called Matthew. It was also about Jesus, but was written by a different disciple and so had some things in it John hadn't included.

Then he asked if I could come back next Thursday at seven o'clock, and I said I could.

We left the study and walked to the front door. Mrs. Grant came out from the sitting room and said good-bye and smiled at me. I didn't see Nicole.

I walked with Pastor Grant to the church. He said he was sorry he had to rush to the meeting and I said I was sorry to make him late.

Then he said, "See you Sunday," and went in.

I walked home slowly, thinking about what I'd done. I still didn't understand it all, but I felt good. Really good.

Next day, Thursday, the story about the fight was all over the school. Of course, it had been garbled beyond recognition, but neither Luke nor Charlie was there to explain.

Friday was the last day before Christmas, and they didn't show up at school then either.

I got through the day somehow and then went home. Mom was next door, so I walked over to the Thorntons' and rang the bell. Mrs. Thornton came to the door.

"Hi. Is Charlie here? I was just wondering how he is."

"You can go up to his room if you want." She didn't smile.

Charlie's bedroom door was open. He had the TV on and he was lying on his bed watching it. He had a black eye and swollen lips and a bunch of bruises.

"Hi," I said from the doorway.

He looked at me, then used the remote control to switch off the set. He sat up, but not without a few grimaces.

"What do you want? Come here to gloat?"

"Nope. Just to see how you are."

"Just fine, thank you."

We eyed each other.

"I know the reason Nicole won't date you," I said at last.

"Oh? Why?" he asked casually, as if he didn't care one tiny bit.

"It's like Paul said. Her dad won't let her. And the reason he won't let her is because you aren't a Christian."

"Which is—?"

"Someone who lets Jesus Christ control his life."

"So what you're saying is he'll only let her go out with one of those religious fanatics like the ones at the retreat?"

"I guess."

"Well, that's okay. I've got other fish to fry right now."

"Yeah?"

"Yeah." He grinned as well as he was able. "Jamie is going to the Christmas dance tomorrow night with me."

"She is?"

"You heard."

"So that's how you decided to get even with Luke! Stealing his girl!"

"You've got it."

"Did Luke know that when he hit you?"

"Jamie had told him right before she met me. Apparently, I should have been smart enough to stay out of his way for a while."

"You likely wanted to gloat."

"Touché."

"Well, have a good time at the dance." I grinned. "Seriously, I do hope you're okay soon." I left without mentioning that I didn't think there was any way he'd be going to a dance the next day.

My next stop was Luke's. It was a long walk, but one I'd made many times.

His mom let me in. "Oh, Glen, I'm so glad to see you. Maybe you can do something with him. His dad's so mad at him, and he won't say he's sorry or anything."

I went up to Luke's room and knocked. No answer. I opened the door. His room looked like a cyclone had hit it. He was lying face down on the bed.

I went in. If he heard me, he gave no sign.

"Hi, Luke," I said.

He jerked up. He could only see a little out of one eye. He looked even worse than Charlie. "Whadya want?" he mumbled out of thick lips.

"You could use a shave. Also a whole brigade of cleaning women and—"

"Shaddup."

"I hear Charlie stole your girl."

He'd have hit me if I'd been closer. As it was, all he hit was the bed.

"Don't worry, Luke. I doubt if he'll be going to the dance tomorrow. He looks nearly as bad as you."

He swore at me.

"Know what, Luke? I think it's the best thing that could have happened."

He swore again.

"No, I really do. You haven't been yourself since you started to date Jamie. You know what I mean. You aren't much fun any more."

He threw his pillow at me. It hit a picture on the wall and knocked it down. Luckily, it didn't break.

"I mean it, Luke. You've lost sight of everything except Jamie. You know, there are other girls around. Some really nice ones, too. Most of them would love to go out with you. You're too young to tie yourself down to one. Let Charlie have Jamie. He'll be the one getting her groceries and carrying her books and driving her where she wants to go and helping her with her homework and baby-sitting and—"

I thought at first he was choking, but when I went closer, I saw he was laughing.

I started to laugh, too.

When his mom came up, we were both sitting on the bed laughing, only Luke was doubled up yelling, "I can't laugh. It hurts!"

I helped his mom change the sheets on the bed and get it all nice and cool and crisp. She helped him wash and get more comfortable.

I talked to him while she cleaned up some of the mess in his room. I told him about seeing Charlie, and how I got the A in physics. He and his mom both thought it was weird my having to give back the money when I got the A.

After his mom went out, I told him about getting stuck in the closet in the Grants' house and how I'd gotten the letter, and how Nicole told me later that she'd seen it and thought I'd written it.

He thought that was pretty funny.

I told him what I thought of him.

His mom came back up to ask if I wanted to stay for dinner, but I said I'd better go. I phoned Mom to say I'd be late. Then I took off—running most of the way.

I felt good. Luke wasn't mad at me anymore, and Charlie wasn't really upset. Life was getting better already.

But there was one more thing I had to do.

After dinner. I asked Dad if I could borrow the car and he agreed. He and Mom were having a few friends in for bridge.

I drove over to the Grants' house. The lights were on at the church next door. I knew the youth group's Christmas party was tonight, so Nicole would be at it. It started at seven-thirty. I checked my watch. Seven forty-five. I wondered who she'd gone with.

But when I rang the doorbell at the house, to my astonishment, Nicole opened the door. She wore jeans and a sweat shirt. She looked nervous. "Hi, Glen," she said. "The party isn't here. It's at the church."

"I know."

"Oh. Well, what do you want?"

"Is your dad here?"

"Yes." She reluctantly opened the door and I went in.

I hadn't realized before how small she is. Maybe I'd never noticed. Dumb, I guess. Now I realized I had to look down quite a ways. Maybe I'd been growing taller.

"I'll get him," she said. "He's only playing chess with Paul."

"I can wait."

She smiled a bit. "Not the way they play. They take hours to make one move."

I laughed.

"You can come in if you want."

"Thanks."

I followed her to the living room. Pastor Grant looked a bit surprised to see me, but he got up and shook hands.

"Sorry to bother you," I said, "but there's something I need to tell you and I—well, I want to get it over with."

"We can go to the study."

"No. It's okay. It involves Nicole, too."

The three of them looked at me. Pastor Grant said, "Well, sit down, then."

"It's sort of complicated," I said. Now that the moment had come, I wished I was anyplace else but here. "You see, when Charlie moved to town, he met Nicole, and, well, liked her." Nicole was looking at the floor. "Only she wouldn't go out with him no matter what he did. He tried a lot of things, believe me." I stopped to breathe.

"Go on," Pastor Grant said.

"Well, he also made Luke pretty sore at him. It was both their faults. Mine, too." I paused again. "Anyway, through a kind of mix-up, somebody put a note in Nicole's math book last week. You remember the day Charlie and I came over?"

Pastor Grant nodded.

"Glen," Nicole said. "Luke phoned me a little while ago and told me about the note."

"He did?" I asked in surprise.

"Actually his mother did. She said he couldn't talk very well yet."

"No, he can't. Well, that makes it easier. Luke put the letter in and then wished he hadn't. So he got Jamie to tell me. Charlie and I came over to see if we could get it before you found it. We saw everybody leave and so we—I—sneaked into the house. The front door was unlocked. I was looking for the note when you came back. I—" I looked down, knowing my face was red "—I hid in the closet in the study."

There was silence. At last, Pastor Grant said, "I see."

"I—I felt I had to tell you. I really feel bad about it. Honest. I've never done anything like that before."

"Why did you want to get the paper before Nicole read it?" Pastor Grant asked.

I pulled the letter out of my pocket and handed it to him. He read it, then looked up. "So you were worried about Charlie looking foolish?"

"Well—I guess so."

"Or perhaps about Luke looking that way?"

"Yeah, I guess."

I looked at Nicole. She had her hand to her face and was steadily gazing at the floor. I continued, "When Charlie came to the front door, I went out the back. Then I came around and asked Nicole something about the math homework. She gave me the book and I got the letter out."

Pastor Grant looked at Nicole. "You hadn't seen it?"

"Yes, I had. I'd found it earlier, and I was just going to tell you about it when Charlie came to the door."

"But you didn't say anything?"

"When Glen asked me about the math questions, I realized he was trying to get the letter. He'd never have come here to ask me for a homework assignment."

"I see. Well, Glen, thank you for coming over here and clearing this up. I appreciate your honesty."

"There's just one more thing, sir. I was trying not to listen, but I couldn't help hearing you and Nicole talking about the party tonight."

Nicole gasped and ran from the room.

Paul laughed, and Pastor Grant asked him to leave.

"I'm sorry," I said. "All I heard was that Nicole wanted

to go with Charlie to the party tonight, but that you wouldn't let her because he isn't a Christian. In fact, it was hearing you say that that got me wondering what a Christian was. So although I'm sorry about what I did, I guess I'm not really sorry it happened. Anyway—"

"You heard Nicole say she wanted to go to the Christmas party with *Charlie?*" Pastor Grant asked.

"Yes, sir. Look, he isn't a bad guy. All the girls seem to go for him."

Pastor Grant was laughing. "Not quite *all* the girls, Glen. What exactly did you hear her say?"

"Well, just that she wanted to go out with somebody who wasn't a Christian, but who was ten times better than Derek. You asked if it was one of those new guys who'd been coming to church, Charlie or—" I blinked. "She *doesn't* want to date Charlie?"

He shook his head. He was smiling.

"But—but then—?"

"You know, Glen, the party's barely started. Still plenty of time to go over. That is, if you want to."

"If I want to? Pastor Grant, there's nothing in this world I'd rather do. But— I don't get it! Why would anybody rather go with me than with Charlie?"

"Why don't you ask her?" Pastor Grant said. He left me sitting there wondering if I had entered an alternate universe.

It was about fifteen minutes before I heard footsteps.

I stood up.

Nicole was standing in the doorway. She'd changed to a dark green sweater and a black skirt, and she looked absolutely gorgeous. Just like Charlie had said.

But Charlie'd missed so much. He only saw what was on the surface. He couldn't seem to see the best things—what she was like inside—gentle, and caring, and sweet. I wondered if Charlie would ever understand.

Nicole was looking at the wall instead of at me. "Dad said you want to go with me. He wouldn't let me ask you before. He wasn't sure if you'd really become a Christian or if you'd just done it because of me."

I shook my head. "No, it wasn't because of you. Not directly, anyway."

"I'm glad. So, would you like to go to the party with me?" Her voice trembled a bit, like maybe she wasn't absolutely certain I'd want to.

I walked over and took her hand. I'd never held a girl's hand before, but it wasn't difficult. "I wasn't planning to go to the party," I said. "I just have jeans on."

"I don't care," she said.

"Then what are we waiting for?"

We walked across the room, her hand in mine. Then we were outside. We walked down the sidewalk and toward the church. She started to go inside, but I held her back. She looked up at me. I could smell the perfume she was wearing. It was just right. Her eyes sparkled different shades of green. Everything about her was just right—exactly what I wanted.

"Nicole," I said softly. "Squeeze my hand."

"What?"

"I want to find out if I'm dreaming or not. No, don't. If I am dreaming, I don't want to wake up."

"Glen, you—"

"Nicole, is it really true?"

"Is what true?" she asked softly.

"That you want to go out with me—not Charlie?"

Her eyes widened. "Not Charlie, not Luke, not Andy, and not anybody else."

"You mean it?"

"Glen, I've always liked you. Ever since we moved here."

"But I'm such an idiot!"

"I don't think so. I think you're the nicest person in town."

"No way," I said firmly. "I am standing beside the nicest person in town."

"You mean that?"

"Oh, Nicole."

"You've never seemed to go for girls at all."

"That's because there was only one girl I ever wanted to be with, and I never dreamed that she'd go out with me."

Nicole smiled, her eyes alight.

I grinned back before opening the door and following her inside.

We could hear laughter and singing coming from the church basement. We went down the steps of the church—our church. I belonged here now, too. With Pastor Grant's and Nicole's help, I'd learn what it meant to live like a real Christian.

I didn't know how I'd do. I didn't even know what would happen tomorrow. Would Charlie ever speak to me again? Would he end up as Jamie's personal slave or would he cause trouble between me and Nicole? Was the fight between Luke and Charlie the end or just the beginning of their conflict? What more would Marta do to get even with Charlie? What would my parents and friends think of my becoming a Christian?

There were so many questions to be answered. But I'd worry about them tomorrow. Tonight belonged to me—to me and to Nicole.

We entered the brightly lit room together.

Thank You

Thank you so much for reading *The Best of Friends*, the first book in my Circle of Friends series. I hope you loved seeing Glen begin to discover who he is, and what he wants in his life. I had so much fun writing this book!

It would be terrific, if you have five minutes, if you could leave an honest review at the store you got it from. Reviews are so helpful for other readers who are trying to decide whether a book is one they might like or not. Books with a lot of reviews also get more visibility.

The Second Book in This Series, *With Friends Like These*, is Available Now.

What will happen when Charlie discovers that Nicole is interested in Glen? Chances are he won't be happy until he finds a way to break them up.

You can find details and links to where you can get *With Friends Like These* on my website.

njlindquist.com/books/wflt

Opening of *With Friends Like These*

Charlie Thornton was probably the only person in our small town who didn't know I was dating Nicole Grant.

That's because Charlie spent the Christmas holidays in England visiting his grandparents and recovering from the fight he'd had with Luke Trent in the middle of Harry's Restaurant.

Of course, I knew Charlie wouldn't stay in the dark long. But I sure didn't expect Luke Trent, my best friend since nursery school, to be the one to bring him up to speed.

As I followed Luke out of history class on the Monday morning we went back to school, he yelled, "Guess you lost this one, Charlie."

Charlie was ahead of us, so when he stopped dead to stare at Luke he caused a bit of a collision among the rest of the students streaming out of the classroom. "What are you talking about? What did I lose? Not the fight I had with you before Christmas!"

I managed to squeeze through the doorway behind Luke, and I tried to escape by going sideways down the hall, keeping my eyes on Luke and Charlie. I didn't get far before bumping into a half-open locker. No big deal, except the belt loop on the back of my jeans caught on the locker's catch.

"Bet you can't guess who dated Nicole Grant during Christmas holidays?" Luke's tone was deliberately provoking.

"Look," Charlie said. "If you've got something to tell me, why don't you just say it?"

They stood in the hallway, Charlie's styled blond locks practically parallel to Luke's dark mound of unruly curls.

"We all know you've done everything possible to get a date with her," was Luke's response.

"Luke, why don't you just go to your next class? You aren't going to start another fight with me." Charlie started walking away.

"Looks like she found a better man." Luke smiled.

I wanted to yell, "Shut up, you idiot!" but of course I couldn't do that without drawing attention to myself—and to my being attached to a locker.

Charlie stopped and glared at Luke. "I heard you tried to date Nicole yourself."

This happened to be true, but it didn't seem to bother Luke. He grinned and said, "When you find out, you're going to feel so stupid!"

Charlie was moving again.

"You're just trying to start an argument," he yelled over his shoulder.

"Glen Sauten, that's who!" Luke's voice was triumphant. "How's that for a nice surprise?"

Several people laughed.

I couldn't see Charlie's face, but I could imagine him rolling his eyes as he said, "Yeah, right, she's dating Glen. Nice try."

"No lie, buddy."

"Nicole went out with Glen," Charlie stated in a matter-of-fact voice. "As if!"

"No joke, man."

"Give it up. He wouldn't even have the guts to ask her."

Luke shrugged. "Maybe *she* asked *him*."

I managed to free my belt loop from the grasp of the locker, and backed carefully down the hall away from them. So what if my next class was in the opposite direction?

"Sure she did," said Charlie. "How stupid do you think I am?"

"Maybe you should ask how many people saw them together during the holidays." Luke looked like a boxer about to land a knockout punch.

"Don't you ever give up?"

"Why should I? It's true." Luke broke out in a mock chant. "Nicole li-ikes Gle-en." He repeated it several times.

At that point, Marta Billing's strident voice rang out. "He's right, Charlie. Nicole and Glen have been seen together. They've even been holding hands and all that mushy stuff."

Several voices mumbled agreement.

An explosive "What?" came from Charlie's direction. It was followed by "That..." and a string of expletives I won't repeat here, with my name tacked onto the end.

Thanks a lot, Luke. I turned a corner and got out of there.

"Yes, she does"— "No, she doesn't" arguments, I didn't know what more to say. But Charlie didn't seem to expect an answer. He stared at me for a long, uncomfortable moment, and then he leaned his elbows on the cafeteria table and stared into space. I eased off my chair and started for the door.

"Where do you think *you're* going?" he growled as he swung around.

I stopped and faced him. "Uh, I thought—you know—that you were finished."

"I'm finished all right. Finished letting you think you're a friend of mine! Finished pretending you're anything except a weasel that doesn't have the brains of a woodpecker. Why I was stupid enough to let you hang out with me since I moved here—! I guess I felt sorry for you. Well, I don't any more!"

In one motion, he stood up and grabbed the front of my shirt. "If I ever catch you with Nicole, you'll find out how it feels to have Charlie Thornton on your case! Got it, creep?" With that, he strode angrily out of the cafeteria.

I took a deep breath and blew the air out. Although I'd known from the first time I dated Nicole that Charlie would be upset when he found out, I really hadn't known how he'd react. I could live with his threats. It was what else he might do that worried me....

Find out how to get this book here:

njlindquist.com/books/wflt/

Extra Items I Hope You'll Like

1. I've included a link so you can subscribe to get my newsletter and keep up-to-date on what I'm working on or publishing.

2. If you'd like to get deeper into *The Best of Friends*, there are Discussion Questions which you could go over yourself or use in a book club or small group.

3. I've also given you a short bio and a list of my published books at the time of this printing.

4. After that, you'll find a personal note from me.

5. Last but not least, I've posted a list of things you can do to help out authors whose books you appreciate.

Subscribe to My Newsletter and I'll Give You Two Short Stories!

Sign up for my occasional newsletters and I'll give you a couple of my short stories in digital format.

In addition to the stories, you'll receive my occasional newsletters with behind-the-scenes information about writing my books as well as advance notice of any new books, relevant blog posts, sales, recommendations for books I've read, and other things that might interest you.

You can unsubscribe at any time.

njlindquist.com/ya-subscribe/

About the Author

N. J. Lindquist is an award-winning writer and blogger whose published work includes eight young adult books, a Christmas play, and many articles and columns. She also edited and published the Hot Apple Cider Books series.

As J. A. Menzies, she writes the Manziuk and Ryan Mysteries and has begun a middle grade fantasy series.

A former high school teacher, homeschooling mother of four, and church leader, N. J. has been teaching others what she's learned since she was young. In 2001, she co-founded a national organization for Canadian writers called The Word Guild, and served as executive director until 2008. She also directed Write! Canada from 2002 until 2012 and has taught workshops for writers across Canada and in the US.

N.J. lives in Ontario, Canada, with her husband Les, close to their four sons and their families.

njlindquist.com/about-me

You'll find links to her Facebook, Twitter, and other social media pages on her website.

Books by N. J. Lindquist

Coming-of-age Novels

In Time of Trouble: a novel about second chances

The Best of Friends: Book 1 of The Circle of Friends Series
With Friends Like These: Book 2 of The Circle of Friends Series
A Friend in Need: Book 3 of The Circle of Friends Series
More Than a Friend: Book 4 of The Circle of Friends Series

njlindquist.com/books/

The Misadventures of Stefan the Stableboy and Princess Persnickety (as J. Alana Menzies)

The Defenders of Practavia

realmofthekingdoms.com

Hot Apple Cider Books (as editor)

Hot Apple Cider: Stories to Stir the Heart and Warm the Soul
        Hot Apple Cider Discussion Guide
A Second Cup of Hot Apple Cider: Stories to Stimulate the Mind and Delight the Spirit
        A Second Cup of Hot Apple Cider Discussion Guide
A Taste of Hot Apple Cider: Stories to Encourage and Inspire
Hot Apple Cider with Cinnamon: Stories of Finding Love in Unexpected Places
Christmas with Hot Apple Cider: Stories of Giving and Receiving

hotappleciderbooks.com

The Manziuk and Ryan Mysteries (as J. A. Menzies)

Shaded Light: The Case of the Tactless Trophy Wife
Glitter of Diamonds: The Case of the Reckless Radio Host
Shadow of a Butterfly: The Case of the Harmless Old Woman
The Case of the Homeless Pup: A Manziuk and Ryan Novella

7 Mystery & Suspense Short Stories, including Paul Manziuk & Jacquie Ryan in "The Case of the Sneezing Accountant"

jamenzies.com

Digging Deeper into
The Best of Friends

1. There are six main characters in *The Best of Friends*: Glen, Luke, Charlie, Nicole, Zoey, and Marta. Then there are several other characters: Jamie, Brandon, Matt and Paul in particular.

    a. Which of these characters did you most relate to and why?

    b. Do you know people like the other main characters in the book?

    c. If you could be any of the characters, which one would you choose to be, and why?

2. At the beginning of the book, Glen is content to let life happen.

    a. Does this make you relate to him or think of him as a wimp?

    b. How much do you think Glen's position as the youngest in a large family contributed to his personality?

    c. Charlie and Marta have no siblings. Luke and Zoey both have a younger sister. Nicole is the oldest of four. Can you see ways their positions in their families have influenced them?

    d. What is your position in your family and how do you think it has affected you?

3. Glen's dad won't let him buy a car, but Luke has one. Charlie's parents gave him a brand new car for his 16th birthday.

    a. Do Luke and Charlie deserve a car more than Glen does?

    b. What do you think of Glen's father?

4. At the beginning of *The Best of Friends*, Glen is frustrated because Luke is busy with his girl-friend, Jamie, and has no time for Glen.

a. Is Glen right to spend time with Charlie?

b. Have you ever been in a similar position? If so, how did you handle it?

c. Have you been on the other side, where you were the one who had no time left over for your long-time friend?

d. How do you think people should handle relationships with friends of the same sex when they enter a new relationship with a friend of the opposite sex?

5. For various reasons, Luke dislikes Charlie on sight, and it doesn't get better. This puts Glen in an awkward position.

a. Do you think there's any way Glen could have kept Luke and Charlie from disliking each other?

b. Do you think there's any way a person can be friends with two people who don't like each other?

6. Many teenagers feel that nothing bad will happen to them—to "other people" maybe, but not them. So they don't wear sunscreen because "they" won't get cancer, or they drive without seatbelts because "they" won't have accidents. Glen and the others knew it was foolish to go into the cave.

a. Is it true that when we break a rule or ignore advice, we're likely to get into trouble?

b. Why do you think Charlie was hanging around closer to the entrance than the others?

7. The cave-in starts Glen thinking about death. His thoughts are also fueled by the illness of Mr. Jackman's son Frank. Plus Brandon lost a sister in an accident not too long before.

a. Some teens, like Glen, have never thought about death. Others have been forced to deal with it. Have you experienced the death of someone close to you? If so, how has that affected you?

    b. How do you feel about death? Is it an enemy, an inevitable conclusion, a friend, the end, the beginning…?

    c. How do you think the cave-in illustrates what's happening in Glen's life?

8. Glen asks a number of people and even looks up the meaning online to try to figure out what a Christian is. Do you think there's more than one possible definition?

9. Nicole's parents refuse to allow her to date someone who isn't a Christian.

    a. Do you think this is fair?

    b. Nicole is frustrated because some of the boys who attend her church don't act as she thinks Christians should. What are some reasons why someone might say he (or she) is a Christian and even attend a church, but not actually be a Christian?

    c. What are some reasons why someone who is a Christian might act in ways that others find inappropriate?

10. Near the end of the book, Glen is in a closet at the Grants' house listening to Pastor Grant and Nicole talk about him and Charlie.

    a. Do you think Glen should have been in this situation? How could it have been avoided?

    b. Think about a time when you were in an embarrassing situation. How did you handle it?

11. Glen finally realizes it's up to him to take responsibility for his life.

    a. Have you yet taken responsibility for your self and your decisions?

    b. What do you think of Glen's decision to give his life to God?

12. Glen decides God wants him to ask forgiveness for eavesdropping.

   a. How hard is it to go and tell someone else the truth and ask for forgiveness?

   b. How necessary is it?

   c. What should we do when God points out something we need to do, even though it's difficult for us?

A Note from N. J. Lindquist

I'm a writer of hope-filled books, stories, and articles for broken people who live in a broken world.

It wasn't supposed to be this way. We were actually supposed to live in a world that made sense, where war and hatred and poverty and prejudice were unknown. Only that obviously isn't the way it turned out, and no matter what country we call home, we live in a broken world.

Since it's impossible to live in a broken world and not be affected by it in some way, we all have parts of ourselves that are broken. But broken things can be fixed. And so can broken people.

I live in hope that, just as this world will one day be remade in the way it was supposed to be in the first place, so the broken parts in each one of us can also be fixed. And we can become everything the One who created the world intended us to be in the first place, when He knit us together in our mothers' wombs.

If you're looking for assurance that you aren't alone, plus a little encouragement, then please hang out with me.

My philosophy is that the only way to heal the broken parts of us and our world is to learn to trust God, to trust ourselves, and to find a group of trustworthy, like-minded people.

There's an old cliché that says it's better to light just one small candle than to sit hopelessly in the darkness. I consider my writing to be my candle.

How to Make an Author Happy

Writing a book is actually a lot of work. Writing a **good** book is even more work.

If you like this book and want to show your appreciation for the effort I put into writing it (thus encouraging me to write more books), here are 4 ways to do it.

1. Write a review. Post your review on bookstore sites, Goodreads, your blog, and/or anyplace else you frequent. It doesn't have to be long. A couple of sentences is enough. (Just remember not to give away the plot!) And do let me know about your review. Even if you said a few negative things, it's okay.

2. Tell other people about my books. Better yet, buy some books and give them to people you think would enjoy them too.

3. Buy my other books. Or get them from your library. If you liked this one, you'll probably enjoy the others too.

4. Connect with me by subscribing to get my reader updates, follow me on Twitter and/or FaceBook, etc.

Trust me, I'll appreciate it very much. The world of a writer can be a lonely one.

Of course, everything I've said above applies to any author whose work you like!

Publisher

That's Life! Communications

Books that integrate real faith with real life

That's Life! Communications is a niche publisher committed to finding innovative ways to produce quality books written by Canadians with a Christian faith perspective.

thatslifecommunications.com